THEIR STOLEN BRIDE

BRIDGEWATER MÉNAGE SERIES - BOOK 7

VANESSA VALE

Copyright © 2016 by Vanessa Vale

This is a work of fiction. Names, characters, places and incidents are the products of the author's imagination and used fictitiously. Any resemblance to actual persons, living or dead, businesses, companies, events or locales is entirely coincidental.

All rights reserved.

No part of this book may be reproduced in any form or by any electronic or mechanical means, including information storage and retrieval systems, without written permission from the author, except for the use of brief quotations in a book review.

Cover design: Bridger Media

Cover photos: Period Images; fotolia.com- Jag_cz

GET A FREE BOOK!

JOIN MY MAILING LIST TO BE THE FIRST TO KNOW OF NEW RELEASES, FREE BOOKS, SPECIAL PRICES AND OTHER AUTHOR GIVEAWAYS.

http://freeromanceread.com

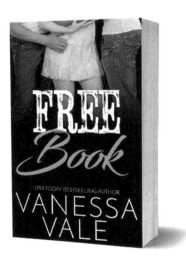

PROLOGUE

ARY

"Up on your hands and knees, darlin'."

The man stood beside the bed, naked as the day he was born, stroking his very hard cock. Clear fluid seeped from the tip and the wicked grin on his face proved he was having a very good time. He was attractive, slim, muscled, and his jaw was darkened by a trimmed beard.

The woman smiled coyly at him and did as she was told. She wore only a blood red corset, the top few stays undone and her abundant breasts spilling out.

I stood in the next room, looking through a small hole, my hands pressed against the wall, watching. Chloe, one of The Briar Rose's many whores, stood beside me, our shoulders bumping, as she watched from her own secret spot.

The whore, now up on her hands and knees, thrust her

bottom out and wiggled it, inviting the man to look at her pussy. While neither was shy and one was a professional, they had a way about them that indicated they'd been together like this before.

I'd been eavesdropping with Chloe over the past few months and could now tell such things. Yes, I knew the more vulgar terms for a man's member, a woman's secret place and more. Cock, pussy, ass, cum. Those words were no longer crude or salacious. I'd visited the brothel, at first innocently enough to bring used clothing as charity through the Ladies Auxiliary, but met Chloe and returned out of friendship. And, admittedly, because I was curious about what went on in a brothel. What went on between a man and woman.

I gasped as the man spanked the whore on the bottom, a bright pink handprint blooming on her pale flesh.

"See, Nora likes it," Chloe whispered.

There was no doubt the whore knew of the peepholes, but the man who'd paid for a tumble with the plump Nora probably did not. They were meant as a safety measure—men were unpredictable and sometimes cruel—but I found them useful for eavesdropping. Miss Rose, the Madame, seemed content with my *reasonably* innocent activities, just as long as I remained in hiding.

"She likes to be spanked?" I whispered back. I could see she did, with her surprised look, then hooded eyes. I liked it too, but I didn't dare say that to Chloe, or to anyone else. The idea of a man's hand striking my bare bottom made me wet between my own thighs, made my pussy clench, just like Nora.

Her pussy was pink and swollen and slick with her arousal. No doubt mine was as well, and I was just watching. I wanted a man to do that to me. Not the man with Nora, but *some* man.

My man, whoever that may be. I wanted to glance coyly over my shoulder at him, see his wicked grin in return. I bit my lip to stifle a moan when he spanked her again, the loud crack of his palm against her flesh resounding through the wall.

I'd seen whores who were pretending with men, acting out their pleasure in exchange for money. But Nora didn't need to feign a thing with him. Instead of putting his cock inside her—fucking her, as Chloe called it—he knelt on the bed behind her and put his mouth... there.

"Oh lord," I whispered. Chloe covered a giggle with her fingers. I looked at my friend, all wild red hair and pink cheeks, and I knew my eyes were wide. *That* was something new to see.

"He likes pussy," she whispered.

I put my eye back to the peephole when I heard Nora's cry of pleasure. He was licking her woman's flesh, sucking on it, nibbling, too. Oh my. His beard began to glisten with her arousal.

"That's it, darlin', come for me," the man said. "Come on my fingers and then I'll fuck you."

"Yes!" Nora cried. The man wiped his mouth with his free hand and slid his fingers in and out of her as she writhed upon them.

It was hard not to squirm as I watched the man give Nora such pleasure. He was so eager to see to her come that he delayed his own need. I wanted that. I wanted a man who put me first.

The man spanked her again. The man's cock was engorged and dripping, clearly in need of his own release. "Now, darlin'. Give it to me now."

Nora did, crying out her pleasure. The look on her face was exquisite. Wild abandon. She thought of nothing but the bliss the man wrung from her body. The man's wicked grin inferred his power over her body.

God, I wanted that. I ached for it. Needed it. But I wasn't a whore at The Briar Rose. I was a copper heiress and I shouldn't even know about fucking. I shouldn't even know the word itself. But I did. Did that make me a wanton? Probably, but my life was so plain, so strict and dull, that visiting Chloe and discovering an entirely new world was the only thing that gave me amusement. Hope.

Hope that there was a man out there who would want me like this man wanted Nora. I wanted to be wild, not stifled. I wanted to allow every one of my secret desires to be shared with someone who would see to them, not crush them beneath the boot of polite society.

I wanted more than I'd ever get with my intended husband. If my father had his way, it would be Mr. Benson and he would *never* spank my ass, or lick my pussy, or even take me from behind as the man was with Nora. Instead, I'd lie on my back in bed, it would be dark and Mr. Benson would lift my nightgown and rut into me, filling me with his seed. It would be awkward and uncomfortable, sticky and messy; I'd see no pleasure. I'd see... nothing.

When the man and Nora had found their final pleasure, both of them vocal about it, Chloe and I turned from the wall. Another whore, Betty, stuck her head into the empty room where we'd been spying. "Mary, your man is here," she whispered.

"Mr. Benson?" My heart skipped a beat at the idea he may have seen me. Highly doubtful, but unnerving nonetheless. "He's here?"

The idea of watching my intended fuck some other woman made me nauseous.

Betty nodded, but she wasn't excited. "Yes, and he's taking a whip to Tess."

Chloe and I glanced at each other and hurried after Betty. Panic filled me at what I would witness through a different peephole, for I knew then and there that if I married Mr. Benson, the pleasure Nora had found would never belong to me.

1

ARY

The surprise hiss of steam made me stumble as I stepped down from the train.

"Careful, Miss Millard," Mr. Corbin said, taking gentle hold of my elbow until I was once again on solid ground. Even in the heat, I could feel the warmth of his touch through my sleeve.

The platform in Butte was busy, many alighting after a long journey from the east. It was the richest town on Earth and would-be miners were eager to find their own vein of copper and strike it rich.

I wasn't quite so eager, for I'd only come from Billings, not Minneapolis or even Chicago, and had lived in Butte my entire life. I was quite familiar with the town and I did not have the hope the others had. Of course, I didn't need to work for money. Not because I was a woman, but because my father had more of it than God. His words, not mine.

So the journey across the Montana Territory was too short, and I was not ready to return to my father and his intentions. While spending the month with my grandmother was far from exciting, it certainly delayed what I assumed was inevitable. I wanted to turn right around and settle back in the train car, watch Butte trundle right on by and continue on to parts unknown.

Mr. Corbin's hand lingered on me a moment longer than perhaps necessary. I turned to look up at the man—one of the two men—who'd been kind and attentive to me during the journey. We'd chatted amiably for hours and they—he and his friend, Mr. Sullivan—escorted me to the dining car for the noon meal so I didn't have to sit alone. It was no hardship to pass the time with two handsome men.

With his blond hair and quick smile, Mr. Corbin no doubt turned heads wherever he went. He'd definitely turned mine. So had his friend Mr. Sullivan. I'd spent hours silently debating which one appealed to me more. Did I prefer my man fair or dark? At ease or intense? Regardless, they'd both been perfect gentlemen. Sadly.

Even now, with Mr. Corbin's hand at my elbow on the station platform, he kept appropriate space between us and was completely solicitous. No one would look twice at his chivalry. Chivalry was good and all, but I ached for the more... intimate attentions a man had for his wife. I wanted that connection, the bond I saw between my friends and their husbands. The secret looks they shared, a gentle caress, even holding hands. I also wanted to be taken with wild abandon. Fucked, as my friend Chloe called it.

But these men saw me as a lady and would not subject me to such wanton behavior. Drat.

Sadly, Mr. Corbin's hand on my elbow was one of the only touches I'd ever received from a man. I wanted more from him, imagined how his skin would feel against mine, not with the barrier of my dress in the way.

"Thank you," I murmured, wishing he'd stroke his hand down my back, undo the pins in my hair, untie the strings of my corset. As a maiden, I would—or *should*—know nothing of what a man could do once that corset was removed, but I did. Not in the practical sense, but I'd seen enough of what went on between a man and woman to want it for myself. It was Chloe who had piqued my interest in all things male and it seemed I had been thoroughly corrupted. I might be tarnished, but I still had my virtue.

If my father knew of my visits to The Briar Rose and of Chloe, of what she'd shown me, I'd never be allowed out of the house. I'd probably be sent to the convent on the outskirts of town, the Ladies of the Immaculate Conception, until he found a use for me.

I also discovered that my sheltered existence came with skewed and preconceived views of girls like Chloe. The auxiliary ladies had said the whores were poor when instead they earned a pretty penny on their backs and did not need the used clothing I'd delivered. I also discovered the men my father had paraded in front of me as possible suitors were not real gentlemen; I'd surprisingly recognized several through the little peepholes about the establishment. What I'd seen would make those Ladies Auxiliary ladies swoon. All it made me was frequently wet between my thighs and eager for a man's attentions.

Because of my spying, I'd seen the real Reginald Benson, the man walking down the station platform in my direction with my father, and he was *not* a man I wished to court. After knowing what he did to Tess, I didn't even want to be on the same train platform. I shuddered at the memory of the whore's screams as she'd been whipped. Fortunately, Chloe had said Big Sam had come to her rescue and she would recover. Mr. Benson had even been banned from The Briar Rose, but that did not mean he'd change his ways. He'd just find someone else to hurt. And if I were married to him....

And yet my father found favor with the man, for they walked toward me together. My father either knew of the man's cruel proclivities or didn't care.

"Oh God," I murmured. My father wanted a match between me and Mr. Benson. They would not be retrieving me from the station themselves—together—for any other reason. Bile rose in my throat at the realization that I was the link connecting the two biggest mines in town together, one owned by each of them.

I wouldn't be going to the convent; I was going to be married to Mr. Benson and soon.

I couldn't let that happen. I couldn't survive the wicked lash of a whip or any of the other horrible things Mr. Benson would do. There would be no help for me, no rescue. No Big Sam. As a wife, I could be beaten—or worse—without any recourse. I'd be property. I whimpered at the idea and grabbed Mr. Corbin's arm.

Yes, it was an impetuous, yet desperate gesture. But in a matter of a minute, they would find me and take me away.

I looked up frantically at the man. "I... I need your help."

Mr. Corbin's eyes narrowed as he looked at my grip on his

arm before searching the area around us for hidden dangers. He tucked me behind him, sheltering me.

"What's the matter, sweetheart?" he asked, his pale eyes finally meeting mine. I swallowed, for he was just too attractive for his own good and quite concerned. His protectiveness did not go unnoticed, nor did the overly familiar endearment.

"My father is here with a man I do not wish to... offer my attentions."

He glanced down the length of the platform. While there was much commotion, I knew he'd honed in on the duo searching for me. I was glad, for once, that Butte was such a busy place.

"One's the size of a pot-bellied stove, the other has slicked-back hair and mustache?" he asked.

I nodded and kept my face averted, shivering at the description of Mr. Benson. Mr. Corbin turned us so his body blocked the approaching men's view of me, affording me a few more moments' reprieve. He was so big I was well hidden behind his broad shoulders and chest. I barely reached his shoulders. I felt protected and oddly safe.

"Yes. There is much to tell and no time, but my father will marry me to him, the one with the mustache."

"You do not wish it." His voice was low and deep, clear and calm, unlike my frantic one. My palms were damp and my heart was pounding frantically in my chest.

I shuddered at the idea of becoming Mr. Benson's wife. "I could not... could not bear his touch."

Mr. Corbin somehow grew taller, more alert. "If he's done something inappropriate, I will kill him."

His sharp-edged words made my mouth tip up in a small smile, but I worried that he was being quite truthful. I didn't fear that he offered to murder someone, but instead found it protective and reassuring.

With a quick peek around Mr. Corbin's shoulder, I saw they were getting closer. "Pretend to be my intended," I hastily said. The idea was preposterous, but the first thing that came to me. It could work. Mr. Corbin was the right age, he was not married —at least he did not mention a wife during our train ride—and was of an appropriate station in society to make it believable to my father and Mr. Benson.

It was his turn to smile. "When someone proposes to me, they should at least get down on one knee."

Pursing my lips, I struggled with his flippancy at a time like this. "My father is marrying me to the man to broaden his mine holdings. I will be the man's third wife; the first died in childbirth and the second disappeared mysteriously."

All amusement slid off Mr. Corbin's face.

"Your assistance will delay what they see as inevitable, but it will allow me time to escape."

"Escape?" he said, his voice cold.

"I stalled by spending the month with my grandmother in Billings, but the men are both impatient. They would not come to the station for me otherwise. It is not in their nature to tend to anyone but themselves."

"You fear him that much?" he asked. His eyes roved over my face as if assessing the truth of my words.

I darted my eyes to the buttons on the man's shirt so I didn't have to look him in the eye as I said, "Fear him?" I nodded my head. "Absolutely. I've also seen him with whores and I know that we are not... well suited. What he desires and what I long for are opposing."

There was no time to elaborate on Mr. Benson's cruelty.

Mr. Corbin's pale brow winged up. "I'd like to hear about what you long for, but at another time." He glanced behind him. "If your father is so eager to wed you to this man, a fiancé is not going to deter him. I recognize your name, sweetheart, and your father's a powerful one in these parts."

My shoulders slumped and tears filled my eyes. He wasn't going to help me. No one would go against Mr. Gregory Millard. As soon as my father found me, I was doomed for marriage to a dreadful man. The very idea of Mr. Benson naked and on top of me, touching me, fucking me, *hurting* me, made me cringe.

"What's the trouble?" Mr. Sullivan alighted the train and stood alongside us. He was Mr. Corbin's travel companion and had joined us in conversation and lunch. His voice was deep and smooth, his shoulders broad and well-muscled. He was a touch taller than Mr. Corbin, and much more intimidating.

Side by side, their large bodies shielded me from the sun, and hopefully from my father.

I knew from the journey they traveled from Miles City and were also getting off in Butte, but continuing on by horse to Bridgewater. I'd heard of the community, which was a few hours' ride from town, but had never met anyone from there before. They'd been pleasant and good conversationalists.

I glanced up at Mr. Sullivan, all dark hair and cool manners. He placed two leather satchels on the ground at his feet. Where Mr. Corbin was cheerful and amiable, Mr. Sullivan rarely smiled. It was difficult to read his thoughts, to discern if he'd found my presence in the dining car a nuisance or not. He just stared, then stared some more. It had been unnerving to say the least, as if the man could see every dark secret I held. In the dining car, Mr. Corbin had slapped his friend on the back and assured me he was just a brooder with everyone.

"Miss Millard does not wish to court the man approaching with her father. She asked that I assist her by playing her intended, but it won't work."

Mr. Sullivan searched the crowd and while I couldn't see, I knew the moment he found them. "Benson. Shit, woman, you're being married Reggie Benson?"

My mouth fell open in surprise and not because of the swearing either. While neither were poor men trying to find a job to survive, they weren't garbed in the finest fashions like the truly wealthy. They didn't seem like the type to associate with Mr. Benson, but it was possible I was in error. Who were these men and was I insane to engage in their assistance?

I cleared my throat and met Mr. Sullivan's dark eyes. "Yes, my father is very insistent on growing his mining empire. Since Mr. Benson owns the Beauty Belle operation, I'm confident of his intentions."

Mr. Sullivan nodded decisively. "Then we should just kill him."

Before I could even sputter a reply at the... violent way both of them wished to solve my problem, Mr. Corbin spoke. "I offered that already."

Mr. Sullivan grunted. "Parker is right, Miss Millard. An engagement will not deter Benson."

So much for my idea. I looked at the ground, dejected. I had no doubt within the month I would be Mrs. Benson. Clearing my throat, I pasted on my best fake smile. I was quite adept at feigning happiness. "Yes, I understand. It was a silly notion. Thank you both for helping me pass the time on the train, gentlemen, but I must—"

Mr. Sullivan cut me off. "An engagement will not deter the man," he repeated. "But a marriage will. Not to Parker. On paper, legally, you should be married to me."

"I beg your pardon?"

"If he is as you say, then I can't, in good conscience, let you marry him."

I flicked a look to Mr. Corbin and he nodded his agreement.

My shock was obvious in my voice. "Yes, but by you marrying me in his stead?"

Mr. Sullivan placed his fingertips on my lips and my eyes widened at the bold touch.

He grinned then, brilliantly and wickedly. "Yes, exactly. Fair warning, I'm not like Benson. I will make demands on you, but I would never harm you. Marry me and I will protect you with my life."

If his fingers hadn't pressed against my lips, my mouth would have fallen open in surprise at his vehemence.

2
———

ARKER

The moment Miss Millard entered the train car in Billings, I knew she was the one. While the porter followed behind her carrying her small bag, she stumbled down the aisle as the train picked up speed. Pitching about, she used her hands on the backs of the seats for balance. I stood immediately, drawing Sully's eyes from the book in his lap to the woman we would marry.

The dress she wore was of the finest cut, in a pale green silk with a bright sheen to it that, beneath my fingers, wouldn't be as soft as the skin on her long neck. I didn't have to be female to know the latest style or the expense of the materials. Her little hat, angled just so on her head of blond curls, matched perfectly. The gown was completely modest, from the long sleeves to the high collar, but it did nothing to hide her enticing curves.

For one so petite—she only came up to my shoulder—she had full breasts and wide hips. She was lush and just a bit shy of plump, but that was how I liked my woman. When she rode my cock—and she *would*—I'd be able to get a good grip on her lush hips. When I spanked her ass—based on her gentle nature it would be more for pleasure than punishment—it would quiver beneath my palm and turn a perfect shade of pink. Her breasts would be a delicious handful and I could only imagine her eyes blurring with passion when I tugged on her hardened nipples.

Stepping forward, I took the bag from the porter, then pulled a coin for him from my pocket. With a quick nod, he turned on his heel and left the car. Placing her bag beneath the seat, I gestured for her to sit across from us. While the car was not full and she could select her own seat, I removed that option for her. Her good manners dictated she accept the placement. Sully respectfully rose to his feet, ducking his head as he was so tall, and gestured for her to join us. As she settled in, adjusting her long skirts, I glanced at Sully. A slight nod was all I needed to know he was in agreement.

Within one minute, our lives changed. Inalterably. This fair-haired beauty would be ours. And so we'd talked with her from Billings to Butte. Well, I did. Sully was not one for many words and passed the time by watching her closely. I noticed the slight turn of her lip when she smiled, every freckle across her nose, the dainty swirl of her ears. We spoke of everything from her staid visit with her grandmother for the past month, to books, to politics in the Montana Territory. She was well versed, clearly well educated. While my cock wanted her for her body,

I was glad she had a sharp wit and gentle spirit inside such a delectable package.

It was easy to fantasize how it would be with her as I listened to her soft voice, imagined how it would sound crying out my name as I brought her pleasure, how she'd beg Sully to take her. Harder. Deeper. Faster.

Fortunately, a surprising herd of elk were visible in the distance. As she watched them, I adjusted my cock, fair near to bursting within the tight confines of my pants. Sully just smirked.

It was then, once we'd pulled into Butte and I helped her down from the train, that I was pleased that she turned to me. At the time, I hadn't known why she'd panicked, but I'd already considered her as mine and I would solve all of her problems. Sully, too. When I discovered who she was, that she was a copper heiress with an uncaring father set on using her for a business deal, my protective instincts took over. When I found out she was to marry that asshole, Benson, I was glad that Sully had joined us.

Benson was ruthless. A callous businessman, he considered money before men. His mine wasn't safe; collapses occurred with dangerous frequency, knowing one dead man could easily be replaced with two more desperate ones. Copper was pulled out at a pace that made him richer than even those who owned the railroad. Assessing Miss Millard's father, I had to guess that he might be even richer.

Men with avaricious business practices used people like pawns, even innocent daughters for marriage alliances. Miss Millard had laughed and warmed to our witty conversation on the train, so I knew she'd become a skittish and fearfully submissive woman if married to Benson. There would be no humor, no caring, no loving. There'd be fucking, surely, but she would not enjoy it, would not feel one bit of desire. Benson had worked his way through two wives and all the whores in Butte. He was infamous for his cruelty—infamous enough that even the innocent Miss Millard knew of it—and only the most jaded and darkly inclined whore could enjoy his needs.

Miss Millard was a passionate woman, I had no doubt. It would be our pleasure to awaken her every desire. To discover what she liked, what made her pant my name, to scream Sully's, as we took her. But only a ring on her finger and her desperate need for our protection from Benson guaranteed that. While she expected a temporary arrangement, in her panic she could not see that *temporary* would not work. An end to an engagement would only delay her father's plans. A *real* marriage was the only way to prevent the inevitable.

A real marriage she would get. Sully, as her husband, would afford her more protection than I would. It was a quick and smart decision, to shift the legal aspects of our union to him. As her husband, he'd protect her from the likes of Benson and her father with just his name alone. With his background, his notoriety, no one would dare impede.

When he'd warned her that he was not like Benson, that he would make demands on her, she would discover what those kinds of demands were, in time. It involved letting two dominant men control her in the bedroom, and quite a few places outside of it. Yes, Benson would have been a controlling spouse, but he would not be loving. From this moment forward, Miss Millard was the center of our world and she was right where she should be—between us.

When Sully lifted his finger from her mouth, he leaned in and said, "Smile, love. You're not alone any longer."

That was correct. She would not be alone again. Would not have to stand up to her father by herself, would not have to associate with the likes of Benson. They couldn't touch her. Not physically, not emotionally.

Being married to two husbands was not the societal norm, especially for Butte. On the ranch at Bridgewater, that was not the case. Everyone was married in such a fashion: two—or more—men for every bride.

"I don't even know your given name," she murmured, offering Sully a quick, nervous glance before facing the approaching men. I watched as her hands fiddled with her dress, that she bit her lip, eyes wide with trepidation.

"Name's Sully." He ran a hand down her arm. "Don't you worry, sweetheart. We'll take care of you. Always."

Taking a deep breath—which made her breasts swell beneath her dress—she rolled her shoulders back and tilted her pert chin as if she were royalty. I could sense her nervousness and fear, but she hid it well. I just had to wonder *why* she'd had to perfect the skill.

Her father and Benson approached, their shined shoes loud on the brick. I knew the moment they first saw Miss Millard—shit, we didn't know *her* given name—but I was even more aware of when they discerned Sully's possessive hold on her.

While her father was short and round, his bespoke suit fit perfectly. His gray hair was thinning and the shiny skin of his scalp was red and freckled from the sun. Loose jowls formed his neck. Along with his hefty weight, he was not a man to deny himself anything. That meant he would not be happy when he learned that Benson would not be marrying his daughter.

Benson was the opposite of Millard. Tall and thin, he had the gaunt look of a man who didn't need to lift a finger. His word, his command, brought immediate results. He, too, was dressed immaculately, in a crisp suit as black as his hair and mustache; he appeared to be in mourning.

"Mary," Mr. Millard said to his daughter.

Mary. The tone he imbued in that one word held so much meaning. None of it was pleasure at seeing his daughter after a month's separation. He did not pull her in for a hug; he did not put a hand on her shoulder for a simple squeeze. He didn't even smile. Mary, though, took a small step closer to me.

"Hello, Father. Mr. Benson." She tilted her head in greeting. "It was very thoughtful of you to meet me at the station, but unnecessary."

"I trust your visit with your grandmother was pleasant."

From what Mary—I liked it much better than calling her Miss Millard—had said about her visit, the woman was definitely this man's mother. She sounded like an old bat.

"Yes, quite."

She could lie to her father, but once we were married, she would be put over my knee if she kept the truth of her feelings from us.

Millard glanced at Sully, then dismissed him readily. I tried to hide a smile, for the man had no idea who Sully was, who he'd just spurned.

"Then we should be going. Mr. Benson is eager to join us for dinner and will escort you home afterward."

Mr. Benson looked at Mary absently, almost clinically, not of a fiancé eager for her return after a month's separation.

Mary shook her head, but Sully spoke for her. "That's not going to happen, Mr. Millard."

Both men deigned him with some attention after all. "And

who are you to dictate Mary's actions? To question my authority over her?"

He offered a small shrug, and I could see he kept his anger at the supercilious man hidden. "I'm her husband, so I believe it is my authority she follows now."

Mary tensed at that, but I knew it was the way Millard thought of his daughter, as a minion who had to follow commands without hesitation.

Millard's skin turned a bilious shade of red and I worried he'd have apoplexy on the train platform. Benson wasn't quite so... internal with his emotions.

If Sully had offered his name, they'd have given a completely different reaction. He didn't and it was telling how they felt about this turn of events.

"I don't know who you think you are, but Mary Millard is my intended." Benson's voice carried on the crowded platform and passersby turned to look.

"Was, Benson. She *was* your intended. She's *married* to me. If you'll excuse us, please."

Sully took a step toward the station's entrance, keeping Mary close, but the man held up his hand. I didn't expect it to end that easily.

"I want proof," Benson said.

I looked at Mary, saw the fear there. Was she worried that Sully would change his mind and give her to these two? There wasn't a chance in hell. To get to her, Benson would have to kill me first, then Sully, because he wouldn't let harm befall her either.

Kissing Mary's temple, Sully murmured, "Tell them, sweetheart."

From where I stood behind them, her scent filled my nose,

all flowery and bright sunshine. I could only imagine how silky soft her hair was against Sully's lips. I was eager to be rid these men and get her alone with Sully, my fingers itching to hold her as well.

"I... I'm married. He's my husband." Her chin tipped up another notch.

Benson offered Mary a quick glance, then ignored her. "That's not the proof I'm looking for."

"Is it the blood on the bed sheet you're seeking? I promise she's well and properly mine," Sully baldly stated.

In a surprise burst of bravery after the discussion of the bloody proof of her virginity, Mary spoke. "He fucked me. Is that what you wanted to know? The first time, he let me be on top. The second time, he couldn't hold back and took me from behind."

Both Benson and her father were as stunned by her words as I was, for they just blinked at her. Where the hell did she learn to talk like that?

"Crude," Benson muttered, as if she were now abhorrent.

I thought she was now even more intriguing than ever. She knew about fucking, but her very demeanor indicated innocence. What was she, harlot or virgin? I wanted rid of these bastards so Sully and I could find out.

"I want the marriage certificate," Benson commanded.

Sully shrugged negligently. He had the power—without even using his infamous name—and wanted to make it clear that they didn't scare him. They didn't scare me either, not in the least, but I didn't want them to scare Mary any more. If lying for her would do it, it made Sully no less a gentleman.

"There is none," Sully told the bastard. "You can check the church register in Billings. First Presbyterian at the corner of

Main and Fourth." Most likely added to irritate the man further, Sully said, "My cock needs relief. You're keeping me from fucking my bride."

Sully dipped his hand about her waist, placing it lower than proper so his little finger brushed over the delectable curve of her ass. It did not go unnoticed.

The stationmaster blew his whistle and the train began to hiss and chug, the noise of the train cars tugging and pulling each other into motion was too loud to talk over. While neither Benson nor Millard had muscle—or guns—they had money and could hire both. Sully's life was on the line now. He knew it. I could see it in their harsh glares. They didn't need to say a thing, to insinuate anything. Before the train was completely away, they'd turned and left. While I wished it was the last I'd see of them, I knew that wasn't to be the case.

Sully moved Mary away so we could both look at her. "Are you all right?"

She tilted her head back and glanced between the two of us, nodded. She took a deep breath, then another. "I appreciate your assistance, but I fear I've probably put you in some danger."

I laughed. "They can try, sweetheart. They can try. I don't think we should stay in town though."

"Mmm, yes," Mary commented. "I'm sure we'll be banned from all hotels, restaurants, even boardinghouses within the hour. My father's reach is vast."

She didn't seem fearful anymore, or angry. Dejected, perhaps.

I glanced at Sully. "We'll go to Bridgewater where it's safe. I assume you have no reason to stay in Butte any longer."

She looked up at Sully and frowned. "You've... you've done

your job. I've gotten both men to leave me alone, and now that they believe we're... intimate, Mr. Benson won't want me anymore."

Sully laughed then. "I still want you, virgin or not. It's not your pussy Benson's after, but your inheritance. For me, it's definitely the other way around."

Her mouth fell open at his crude words. She was definitely a virgin. I'd bet fifty dollars on it.

"There's no chance we're leaving you here in Butte to fend for yourself," Sully added. "You'll be married to Benson at first light if he gets his hands on you, and that's only going to happen if we're dead. I said I'd help you, that I'd be your husband and I'm following through with it."

"That's right, sweetheart," I added, running a gentle hand up and down her arm, shifting so she stood between us, right where she belonged. "You're stuck with us."

"At Bridgewater, we'll be prepared if your father or Benson sends men," Sully added.

"Oh God, he'll kill you to get to me." Color leached from her face.

I took hold of her shoulders and stooped so we were eye to eye. "He'll try, but he won't succeed. Do you doubt that Sully and I can take care of ourselves, that we can take care of you?"

She looked over her shoulder at Sully, then back at me. "No."

I smiled then. "Good girl."

"The sun's setting and we have no supplies," Sully commented.

"Which I doubt we'll be able to collect. Horses, either," I added. If Benson and Millard had their way, we'd be banned from every business, livery or even a Chinese laundry by morning. They had their own kind of power.

"We need a place to stay tonight. Someplace safe. Someplace they'll never look," I added, looking to Sully for ideas.

Mary turned on her heel and started walking. The platform was practically empty now that the train was gone and we caught up to her quickly with our long strides.

"I know just the place," she said. "Gentlemen, how do you feel about whores?"

3

ULLY

"Sweetheart, you've got some explaining to do," I leaned down and whispered in Mary's ear.

She'd led us across town to the back door of The Briar Rose brothel. There hadn't been enough time for Millard or Benson to send out some goons to harass us so our walk had been uneventful. I hated Butte. Any city for that matter. There were too many people, too many ways to get in trouble. I went out of my way to avoid trouble, but today, it happened upon us in the form of a blond-haired vixen. Oh, she was innocent all right, but she tempted me—and Parker—all the same. There had been no question that she was the woman for us, problems and all.

So instead of avoiding conflict or any chance of additional strife in my life, I accepted Mary's as my own. What troubled her, troubled me. What was intending to hurt her, I took care of. There was no way she could be anything but my wife. With my fucking history, I was the safest choice for her. No one would bother her based on being married to me alone. But Mary seemed to lead us from one surprise to another. What virgin miss knew about the kitchen door of a brothel? What innocent was welcomed within with a familiarity that proved she'd visited before?

"A brothel?" Parker asked.

While neither Parker nor I had been to this particular establishment before, it was much like any other. In the past, we entered by the front door. Tonight, we found ourselves gaining entry off the alley and into the crowded kitchen. The cook was stirring something that smelled an awful lot like boiled cabbage on the stove. Two whores sat at the large table in just their corsets and petticoats eating. Another girl came into the room, saw Mary, then fled.

Mary said hello to one of the whores and refused a bowl of the cabbage from the cook. How the fucking hell was Mary mixed up with a brothel? By the way she'd behaved on the train and her complete distaste and obvious fear of Benson, I'd have bet anything that she was a virgin. But what virgin was on a familiar level with those in a brothel?

A woman in just a snug corset and bloomers came through the swinging doorway. Piano music followed her, but was muffled when the door closed. She was of middle height with full breasts almost spilling from the corset. Her legs were long and shapely, her skin creamy and pale. It was her fiery red hair that set her apart from other women. Clearly a whore, she was most likely very successful in drawing attention.

"Mary!" she cried, running over and pulling our bride—we

would be married before the night was through—into a boisterous hug.

They grinned and clearly knew each other. With one blond and the other a redhead, there was no family resemblance. They were not related. How did these two women, from completely different backgrounds, become friends?

"I... need your help," Mary admitted.

The woman glanced at Parker and me. We were big and looming and the kitchen felt small with us in it. She waggled her eyebrows. "I'll say."

When her friend's giggling subsided, Mary made introductions. "This is Mr. Corbin and Mr. Sullivan. Gentlemen, may I introduce my friend, Chloe?"

We removed our hats and nodded. Between Parker and me, I was the quieter and much more patient one, and even he wasn't pushing Mary into giving answers. There were too many, but they would come. If not, we'd spank them out of her readily enough. I doubted anyone in the building would take offense if I sat down and put her over my knee, tossed up her skirts and turned her perfect ass a nice shade of pink.

"We need a place to stay tonight," Mary told her friend.

Chloe eyed Mary closely. "I'll need to get Miss Rose."

She turned on her heel and left before Mary could say more than, "But—"

As we waited, I tugged her over to the back stairwell where there was a hint of privacy. With the stairs at her back and the two of us looming over her, Mary had no choice but to focus on us.

"Explain," I said.

Only one word, but the tone was clear. Mary *would* answer.

She licked her lips and looked up at both of us through her

lashes. "I'm part of the Ladies Auxiliary and over a year ago, I had the task of bringing charity—clothing, mittens and the like—to The Briar Rose. I met Chloe then and we became friends."

My eyes widened as she spoke. "No one from the auxiliary knew you made return visits?" I asked.

"Or your father?" Parker added.

She shook her head. "My father doesn't usually pay me much attention at all. His appearance on at the train station was an odd occurrence. That's why I knew how serious his intentions are. I knew he wanted me to wed, had an idea it might be Mr. Benson, but I wasn't sure until we arrived. That's why I went to visit my grandmother." She shuddered. "My father's mother. You can probably imagine how enjoyable that month was." She sighed. "But it was better than whatever machinations my father was planning. It was a delay tactic, but I am just a woman and do not have any true options."

Her admission was telling of her situation; a woman's freedom was limited, no matter how much money she had. While she didn't have to work, she was trapped doing her father's bidding, or once married, her husband's.

"You are not *just* a woman," I told her. "We're standing in a fucking brothel. I have a feeling there are depths to you that we will have to plumb."

Like her mouth, her pussy, and someday soon, her ass, but Mary didn't discern the double entendre in my words.

A woman cleared her throat. Parker and I stepped back and faced the woman who was definitely the Madame and I assumed Miss Rose. She wore a dress that rivaled Mary's for its taste and quality. She was in her thirties, with fine lines on her beautiful face. From her shrewd assessment of us, I had to assume that not much got past her inspection.

"Mary Millard, when Chloe said you had two men with you and were requesting an upstairs room, I about fainted dead away."

Mary stepped forward, looking contrite. I didn't know if Mary had a mother or not, but the way she was being scolded, I had no doubt this woman could be a replacement.

"You are a good girl. While you peek through the peepholes to ease your curiosity, this is beyond the pale and certainly not like you."

Mary tilted her chin and I could see her cheeks were a bright red.

"I—We had nowhere else to go."

Miss Rose snapped her fingers and the girls at the table stood and left. The cook went out the back door so the five of us were alone. While Chloe stood quietly, she was avidly listening.

"You wish to hide an affair with two men by coming here?"

Mary's mouth fell open. "What? No!"

Miss Rose pursed her lips. "Explain."

The corner of my mouth ticked up as she used my exact word from minutes earlier. We were very similar, not ones to use long sentences when one word would suffice. It boded well for our marriage if Mary responded well to my short and quick commands, for she would learn that Parker and I would be in charge. Not only in the bedroom—or anywhere else we fucked her—but in her safety and well-being, too. Like now, Miss Rose was assuring to her well-being. A good girl like Mary didn't bring two men to a brothel so she could spend a quick hour in a naked tussle.

Mary gave a succinct recounting of her plight, Miss Rose listening intently.

"It was a smart decision, for Mr. Benson has been banned

and knows he cannot gain entry. As for your father, he enjoys the ladies to come to him," Miss Rose replied and I saw Mary squirm at that unpalatable mention of her father. "You are welcome here."

Mary smiled and turned toward the stairs.

"Wait," Miss Rose said, holding up her hand. Mary turned back, waiting anxiously.

"Gentlemen, what are your intentions toward this woman? I assume you are not dolts, therefore know she is not a whore."

"No, ma'am, she's not," I told her. "We intend to marry her."

Chloe and Miss Rose said at the same time, "Both of you?"

Miss Rose was not stunned in the least, while Chloe looked like she'd never heard of a ménage before. In her profession, there was not much she hadn't seen, I was sure.

"Both of you?" Mary repeated.

"Yes, both of us. We told you as much at the train station," I added.

Mary frowned. "You said you'd be my temporary husband, that's all."

I slowly shook my head. "We said we'd take care of you, that we'd protect you. That means marriage. Like Miss Rose said, you're a good girl and will remain as such until we're wed. Then we'll show you how to be a bad girl." I couldn't help but grin at all the wicked things we'd show her. And she'd love them all.

Her mouth fell open in astonishment.

"These men?" Chloe asked. She patted Mary on the shoulder. "Don't worry, honey. They're as handsome as can be. These two will make it good for you. Trust me, you're going to like two men at once."

She giggled then and Mary flushed even darker.

"You must be from Bridgewater," Miss Rose surmised, glancing between the two of us.

I nodded. While we did not make our customs public knowledge, it did not surprise me that Miss Rose knew. She held secrets probably better than even the priests at the Catholic Church and I did not fear she would change her ways now. Surely, she held more... tantalizing confidences than a woman being married to two men who were faithful and loving.

"Then I approve," she added with a decisive nod.

Mary finally claimed her voice. "Miss Rose, you can't mean that you think marrying *two* men is a good idea!"

"I do," she replied. "These are difficult times and Butte is a rough town. It's hard to be a woman in these parts. Even with your money, you were never happy. Why else would you come here? These men want you. Both of them. Some women dream of one man to protect them, but you have the good fortune of two."

Mary stepped closer to Miss Rose and whispered, "But... *two*. I've never seen... I don't know what to do with two."

The older woman smiled then. "Don't worry. I have no doubt they do."

4

ULLY

Yes, we certainly did.

"But—"

Miss Rose held up her hand. "If you wish to spend the night here with these men, you *will* marry first."

Her ultimatum pleased me immensely. It would get our ring on her finger so we could truly protect her from Benson and her father. We could do nothing until she legally belonged to us and I wouldn't tarnish her virtue by expecting anything less.

"But... all the girls. None of them marry the men they take upstairs!" Mary's voice rose as she became upset. "Why me?"

"Are you a whore?" Miss Rose asked bluntly.

Mary looked away. "No," she whispered.

"Then you will marry. I will not allow you to accept anything less. If your mother were alive, she would agree."

The idea of Mary alone with her father, of his ruthless plans for her, made me even more eager to get this wedding done.

Mary looked at both of us. "I... just met you today," she admitted. "How can you be so sure of this?"

I moved to stand directly in front of her. If she took a deep breath, her breasts would touch my chest. I ran my knuckles down her soft cheek. Her eyes closed and she tilted her head into the touch.

She wanted us; she was just too innocent to understand what she was feeling. It was overwhelming and fast, but *right*.

"You've known Benson for quite some time. Length of acquaintance does not guarantee a good match."

Chloe patted her arm. "It's true, honey. Sometimes you just have a connection. When you do, grab hold of the man—or men—and never let go."

Mary didn't seem swayed all that much, but she surprised me when she tilted her chin up, looked at Parker, then at me.

"I won't marry a man... or men, who cheat. Visiting Chloe here over the past year has opened my eyes to the number of married men—men I know from church even—who are philanderers. I can't abide by that." She crossed her arms over her chest and stared at Miss Rose. "You can't force me to marry them if that is the case."

She was adamant and fiery about her opinion and while I should have been offended by her negative assumptions of our honor, I respected her for it. Miss Rose couldn't argue; clearly, she only wanted the best for Mary and that was not a cheat for a husband.

"Mary." Parker put his hand on his chest, directly over his heart. "You're ours. While you'll be legally wed to Sully, you will be my wife, too. I will want no other. I swear I will be faithful."

"As do I," I added.

Mary angled her head toward me. Her mind was working, debating, considering.

Miss Rose looked at us, then at Mary, waiting.

Mary's eyes held no confusion, no fear, nothing but determination as she considered our vows. These words were more important than the marriage ceremony that was to come.

"All right." She nodded her head, as if she needed that gesture to accompany the words. To me, her declaration was enough. "We can't go to the church. My father will know."

Miss Rose waved her hand through the air. "Your father may be powerful in this town, but I have connections." She angled her chin toward the door to the front parlor. "Out there is Judge Rathbone. I have no doubt he'll be happy to preside over your nuptials."

The way Miss Rose worded the last, I assumed she would *entice* the judge into participating.

Chloe dashed out of the kitchen, much more eager for this wedding than the bride.

It didn't take long for the judge to appear, being dragged within against his will by Chloe. For one so small, she was quite strong. The judge was in his fifties and quite gray, overweight and had short, stubby legs. He was missing his suit jacket and his tie was askew, as if he'd been occupied before he was pulled away. He took in the three of us and his eyes widened at the sight of Mary.

"Miss Millard," he said, his words full of surprise.

"I'm sure this little ceremony will be something we all

forget, won't it, Judge?" Miss Rose asked, her voice as sweet as honey. "Isn't your wife on the Ladies Auxiliary with Miss Millard?"

The judge's jowls wobbled as he nodded.

"Then I'm sure Miss Millard and these men will keep secret not only your presence here at The Briar Rose but the things you've done tonight with Elise?"

The judge's eyes widened slightly. He swallowed, thinking about the repercussions. Rolling his shoulders back and taking on a more judge-like bearing, he said, "Who is the groom?"

I stepped forward and took position beside Mary. "I am."

Just this morning I had no idea I would marry. But here I was, with Parker beside me. We were committing our lives to this woman and there was no going back. I glanced down at Mary; she looked calm and... beautiful. Her blond hair was still as neat as a pin, her dress crisp and her hat still at the perfect angle. She looked completely unaffected by the past two hours, completely resolute. I was, too.

"Good," the judge said, glancing at Parker. "You brought a witness."

I was not going to clarify that he was much more than a witness, for I did not want all of our secrets to be shared. I felt confident that the man would not go blabbering about the Millard heiress' secret wedding, for whatever he did with Elise had to be quite licentious to ensure it. But that didn't mean I wished for him to have anything to hold over us.

The judge looked to me. "While I know Miss Millard, please state your name."

"Adam Sullivan."

The man's eyes widened and he swallowed visibly. "Adam... Sullivan?" The judge practically squeaked the last and took a small step back. Mary looked up at me, a frown creasing her smooth brow. It was obvious she did not know me or what I'd done. "Gregory Millard's daughter is marrying Shooter Sullivan?"

I took a step toward the judge and the older man cowered. Yes, he knew of me well. "Is there a problem, Judge?"

The judge shook his head so hard his lips quivered.

Miss Rose's eyebrow winged up and then she laughed. "This is... excellent."

Mary frowned. "What? I don't understand. Do you all know each other?"

"Your husband-to-be is quite famous in these parts. An outlaw, some say," Miss Rose informed Mary. Her shrewd gaze flicked up to me. "How many of your own men did you kill?"

She didn't look horrified by my dangerous past, instead quite amused.

"Four," I replied, stepping back and immediately taking hold of Mary's elbow.

She tried to retreat, but I would have none of it. Without the details, my actions sounded horrific, and I could only imagine what she was imagining.

I'd been part of the US Cavalry and some of the men had gone rogue, taking Indian relations into their own hands. When I'd come upon the men raping and killing at one Indian encampment, I'd defended the innocent. I shot the four men before they could do any more harm. They weren't army men, they were bastards who preyed on the weak. They'd been sick in the head and I'd kill them all over again.

Before the inquest, I'd been painted the enemy, instead of the men who'd done such horrible deeds. Ultimately, I'd been cleared, but released from service. They'd considered me a danger. After that, the story of what I did spread and changed, making me into an aggressive beast of a man, killing anything and anyone that angered me.

Thus, the judge's fear, for he believed the tall tales. In this instance, I was glad the man was so afraid, for he had much more at stake—at least he assumed so—than his wife discovering his infidelity.

I didn't care about the stories or the legend I'd become. I wanted a quiet life, a simple life. And I'd have it, if we could just get the judge to get on with it. But Mary's fears needed to be allayed. I wouldn't have her afraid of me.

I looked down at my fearful bride, tried to soften my voice. "There is much to tell you, and now's not the time with such an audience. But those four men, they were hurting, killing innocent people. I stopped them. As for you, you never have to fear me. *Never.* Isn't that right, Miss Rose?"

I kept my eyes on Mary, not wanting her to think I was hiding anything. I held my breath, for I knew how my past continued to return to the fore and be a nuisance. To tear Mary away from me because of it was something else entirely.

Miss Rose nodded. "That's right, doll. If Sullivan's your husband, you'll never have to worry about your father again. About anyone. You're safe with him. Right, Judge?"

Mary wouldn't have to worry about her father any longer because the man would be too afraid of me to do her harm. If someone dared hurt her, it was our job, our privilege, to make her happy.

The judge shut his mouth, which had been hanging open, and nodded. "That's right. Mr. Sullivan knows how to protect you."

Mary bit her lip, debated. Her face was so expressive. While

I could see no fear in her pale gaze, she was confused and nervous. Both of those things could be resolved soon enough. She just had to accept my word. To accept me, just as I was. I was a patient man, but it was hard to wait for Mary's decision. Only when the ceremony was complete and we had her alone would she discover how devoted we were.

Taking a deep breath, Mary nodded. "All right."

Fuck, I was relieved. To have been rejected by the woman whom I'd promised to protect would have been crushing. She believed in me, enough to marry me. I couldn't help but grin. I released her arm and stroked my knuckles down her cheek once again.

"Good girl," I murmured, and she smiled, her cheeks turning pink at the praise.

The judge began the ceremony, spoke the words quickly he knew by rote. This would be a very short ceremony. The judge wanted it done. I wanted it done. I was sure Parker had been nervous there for a bit as well. Surely, he wanted Mary as ours as soon as possible, too.

She was so beautiful, so self-assured, standing beside me. She accepted her fate, accepted that this was what was best for her, that *we* were the best for her. I was so proud of her, so in awe of her strength.

When the vows were said, I leaned in and kissed her, chastely and quickly, but not before feeling the softness of her lips or hearing the little gasp that escaped. Mary had closed her eyes and when she opened them, they were blurred with newfound passion. It was a heady moment, knowing I'd made her look that way. I could only imagine how she'd look when I *really* kissed her.

"Thank you, Judge." Miss Rose patted the man on the arm

in a placating gesture. He seemed relieved it was over and pulled a handkerchief from his pocket and wiped his sweaty brow. "Please tell Elise that your drinks tonight are my treat."

The man didn't linger, but fled the kitchen at a pace that belied his size.

Miss Rose smiled. "Congratulations, Mary. You may not believe me, but you have a fine husband. *Two* fine husbands. All men from Bridgewater are honorable. Loyal. Loving."

Mary nodded, but had no basis to offer a response. Besides, she looked a little overwhelmed. The deal was done. It was legal. She belonged now to me. And Parker.

"Go up those stairs, the second room on the left." Miss Rose pointed upward. "I think, gentlemen, that you will find it suitable for tonight."

Miss Rose took Mary's hand and gave it a quick squeeze of reassurance, before following in the judge's wake, dragging Chloe along with her, who winked just before the door shut behind her.

"Alone with our bride in a Butte brothel," I said, the corner of my mouth tipping up.

Parker laughed, took Mary's hand. I was sure he felt as relieved as I, knowing she was ours. Officially, legally, permanently. "Whatever shall we do?"

5

ARY

Every visit to The Briar Rose I'd been stunned, amused, even awed by what I'd witnessed, but now, I was a little afraid. I'd felt separate from it all, in a separate room, hiding and watching. A voyeur. From what Chloe said, I was someone who liked to observe others in very compromising situations. It was arousing. Sometimes not. But when a couple did things together that were intriguing, I found my skin heating, my nipples tightening and my pussy getting wet. I dreamed about it. Longed for it for myself. But that had all been fantasy.

Now...now I had two husbands who were eyeing me with an eagerness I recognized. For the first time, that desire was directed squarely at me. Watching was one thing, but *doing*... I was afraid of what they thought of my curiosity and would find me either lacking or a slattern.

Perhaps both, for I'd brought these men to a brothel! It had been my first thought, the first place that I knew neither my father nor Mr. Benson would consider looking for us. My father never knew I had been to the establishment for the auxiliary and would never imagine me going voluntarily. I had not considered the ramifications of my quick decision—obviously, since I was now married and had two eager husbands wanting to consummate the marriage.

I refused to look them in the eye, afraid I would see shame on their faces.

"Mr. Sullivan—"

With a finger, he tilted my chin up so I was forced to meet his dark eyes, the heat I saw in them a surprise. He was so handsome. So tall, his hair dark and unruly and I was eager to run my fingers through it.

"Since I'm your husband, I think you can call me Sully."

"Sully," I repeated.

"No more Mr. Corbin either. I'm Parker, to you." His voice was gentle, tender even.

"What you two must think of me." I felt my cheeks heat.

Parker frowned. "Think of you?"

I wrung my hands and tried to look away, but Sully would have none of it. I was forced to keep his gaze as I admitted my failings.

My heart pounded, my original brashness having fled. "We're going to spend our wedding night in a brothel!"

"You just discovered I killed four people. I have to wonder what you think of me," Sully admitted, letting me go.

I looked at him. *Really* looked. While he was stunningly handsome, he was also very big and physically strong. I had no defense if he wished me harm. On the train—had that only been a few hours earlier?—he'd been quiet, yet solicitous. He'd been gentle as he'd guided me to the dining car, attentive in conversation and watchful for any harm that might befall me. I'd felt safe with him. Discovering he'd killed men while defending the weak hadn't been as surprising as I'd expected. If someone had intended harm upon my person while we were traveling, I had no doubt Sully would have defended me at whatever measure necessary. For him to mete final justice to those deserving was part of his character.

"Miss Rose thinks highly of you. I trust her judgement," I replied.

His dark brow lifted. "Her judgement is enough?"

"We barely know each other and I have to rely on friends to help guide me. You have Parker. I'm sure that you have bigger faults than protecting those in danger."

His dark eyebrows rose even further in surprise.

I clasped my hands together, wrung them. "My father. He's a churchgoer, a millionaire, business owner. A pillar of the community. He was going to *marry* me to Mr. Benson in exchange for some arrangement with their mines. Then there's Mr. Benson. He came here." I pointed at the floor to indicate the brothel. "He... hurt a girl using a whip. A whip! And did other things. Things I knew he would want with me. Or, or he'd do nothing with me. Just get me with child—a boy, of course—then ignore me. If I didn't give him a boy, I would always worry I'd die like his former wives. So being with someone who's killed isn't the problem, but the motivation behind it."

"So you chose the only alternative available?" Parker asked.

I narrowed my eyes. "I only asked for temporary assistance from you. You two were the ones who disagreed with that.

Sully's the one who said he'd marry me. And now, now you say I'm married to you as well."

Parker grinned. "That's right. The judge may have legally bound you to Sully, but my vow from before stands. I'm yours as much as you're mine."

Sully nodded. "You *are* the one for us."

I frowned. "I don't know how you can be so adamant."

Parker put his hand on my shoulder and I looked up at him. "Sometimes you just know." He put his hand to his chest. "Here."

I understood what he meant, for my heart had leapt at my first sight of Parker when he'd stood to relieve the porter of my bag. He'd made my palms damp and I'd been instantly nervous. Then I saw Sully and I'd practically swallowed my tongue. That both men would have so much interest in me for the entire journey into Butte had been surprising and confusing, but I'd reveled in it. Once I'd calmed myself. What woman wouldn't swoon at the idea of two men's focused attentions?

I'd never been so attracted to a man, to two men, ever. Seeing men and the whores come together at the brothel had aroused me, but none had made me jealous of one of my friends. I knew I wanted to do those things with someone... I just didn't know who. Until now.

"But... but both of you? How does a marriage with two men work?"

Parker came forward and pulled me into his arms. His body was hard with muscle and I could feel the beating of his heart beneath my palm. Steady and consistent, perhaps quite a bit like the man himself.

"It's the Bridgewater way. We met a few of the men from

there in the army and they all followed the custom of sharing a bride. If something befalls one of us, sweetheart, you'll still be safe, protected by the other. You're the center of our world now."

Parker relinquished his hold to Sully and he hugged me next. The feel of him was different. They were both tall, both well-built and solid with muscle, but Parker's hold was gentler, while in Sully's arms I felt sheltered. They smelled differently and distinctly. I liked the way both of them held me. I was glad I didn't have to choose one, didn't have to live my life without knowing both of them.

I could only nod in agreement, for I didn't completely grasp this arrangement and my feelings on it. It was so overwhelming, so confusing. So... insane!

"As for the rest, while you are a virgin, you are not completely innocent," Sully said.

I stiffened in his hold.

"You wondered what we thought of you for bringing us to a brothel?" Parker asked.

"The things I said to my father—"

"Like being on top while fucking or being taken from behind?" Sully added. "We haven't forgotten."

I bit my lip and rubbed my cheek against Sully's chest as Parker grinned. *Grinned!*

"I had to say *something*."

"It was a wise choice. Coming here was a wise choice. We're safe and we can spend our wedding night taking care of you, not worrying about your father or Benson. I'd prefer not to sleep with my gun tonight. It's the perfect place to make you ours."

I stiffened in Sully's hold. "Now?" I squeaked.

Parker stepped behind me, moved in close so that I felt his body heat, but not close enough to touch. His hands hovered over my arms and I anticipated his hold, held my breath for it. I was eager to feel Sully on one side of me and Parker on the other.

"Tonight, yes," Parker replied, murmuring in my ear. A chill ran down my spine at the hot feel of it on my neck. "But we aren't brutes. We'll take you only when you are ready."

"But... but what if I'm not ready?" I whispered, gripping onto the fabric of Sully's shirt.

Sully tilted my chin back and leaned down for a kiss.

"It's our job to make you that way," he murmured, an inch from my mouth.

My eyes fell closed at the second kiss of my life. It was as gentle as the one sealing our marriage ceremony, but this was... more. His lips brushed over mine, nibbling and tasting from corner to corner, then his tongue flicked over my bottom lip. I gasped and he took advantage and dipped his tongue inside.

Sully's hands cupped my jaw and he angled my head so he could kiss me as he wanted. Slow didn't mean any less pleasurable, for I felt as if he were learning me, discovering what I liked, what made me make small sounds in the back of my throat.

Parker's hands finally touched me, sliding up and down my arms, then to my waist. With him pressed against me, I felt every hard inch of his broad chest, felt the press of his cock against my back.

I was glad for his hold about my waist for surely I would have melted to the floor.

"My turn." Parker's words broke through my foggy brain and before I could do more than gasp, I was spun about and

Parker's mouth was on mine. Oh, he was a good kisser. Completely different than Sully, but just as arousing. When his tongue plundered my mouth, I tasted peppermint.

Parker growled; I felt the rumbling of it against my palms. When did I put my hands on his chest?

With one last nibble on my bottom lip, Parker lifted his head and stepped back. My eyes fluttered open and I swayed, missing their touch, the feel of them. Their scents swirled together and teased me. *They* teased me and now I wanted more, just as they said I would. If they kissed like that, I wasn't quite as skeptical about the idea of having two husbands. If this was how they could make me feel by just simple kisses... I could only imagine what they could do with our clothes off.

"You'll be ready," Sully said, his voice deeper than normal. He was not unaffected either, for he adjusted himself and I couldn't miss the thick outline of his cock against his trousers.

"Um... I see." I couldn't think of anything else to say, for I believed him to be right. My thoughts were muddled, my body warm and loose, my nipples hard and aching. I wanted them already, my fingers itching to touch them, to learn every hard inch of them.

Parker came around in front of me so they stood side by side. Of similar size, one was fair while the other dark. They were both thickly built, with muscles that couldn't be missed beneath their clothing. So appealing, so handsome and so mine.

"Chloe seems an amiable friend," Parker commented. "What did she teach you?"

I frowned. "Teach me?"

"You visited here several times?" Sully asked.

I nodded.

"Did she take you upstairs?" Parker added.

I licked my lips. "Yes."

"Did she kiss you like Sully did? Undress you? Touch you?"

I gasped at the appalling question. "What?" I shook my head. "No, of course not. That's—"

"Not for you?" Sully replied.

"I... I didn't know. I mean, I never thought..."

"You're not interested in making love to another woman then."

My eyes widened at Parker's words. "I'm a virgin," I said, tilting my chin up. I didn't want them to question that.

Sully smiled. "That's good, sweetheart, but you can find pleasure without losing your maidenhead. And with a woman."

I thought of everything I witnessed through the secret peepholes and it had *never* been two women together. The thought had never occurred to me.

"Oh," I replied, gnawing on my lip. "You're wondering what I learned from watching, besides my crude vocabulary."

Parker reached out and pulled the pin from my hat, removed it from my head. Reaching behind him, he absently placed it on the table beside a bowl of cabbage.

"You watched people fuck?" he asked.

My cheeks flamed and I lifted my hands to them. That word... fuck, was used by Chloe and everyone at The Briar Rose in such a nonchalant way that I'd become immune. But when Parker used it in a question directed at me, I was instantly embarrassed.

My lack of response was answer enough. Both men glanced about.

"You couldn't have gone out into the main rooms," Parker said.

"Of course not," I sputtered. Besides being unseemly, my virtue would have been in tatters and news of my presence spread through town like wildfire. It was acceptable for a man —even a married one—to seek out a woman for a night of passion, but the same could not be said for a woman interested in the attentions of a man. Especially the Millard heiress.

"Where did you watch?" Sully asked, his voice deeper than I'd heard before. Commanding.

Compelled to respond, I pointed to the wall where a hideous painting of a bowl of fruit hung off kilter.

Sully skirted the table and lifted the artwork from the wall to reveal a small hole. Bending down—it was created for much shorter interlopers—he put his eye up to it. I could only imagine what he was seeing in the parlor. After a minute, he stood and moved out of the way, letting Parker take a peek. He groaned at whatever was happening.

He turned from the hole and looked down at me, grinning wickedly. "You were curious about what you saw? Enough to come back more than once. Admit it, sweetheart. There is no shame."

"Yes." I could lie, but it would be pointless.

"Are you curious enough to try the things you saw, now that you're married?"

I turned away, paced across the room, saw that the cabbage was boiling too heavily and adjusted the flame beneath.

"Mary," Parker prompted, my delay obvious.

I stood and spun to them, my nerves getting the best of me. "I don't know how to answer. Either way and you'll think less of me."

Sully came around the table, pushing one of the chairs in as he went. "How so?"

I lifted my hands, let them fall. "If I tell you I'm curious, that I liked what I saw, then you'll think me a loose woman. If I tell you I don't like any of it, you'll think me frigid."

Sully closed the remaining distance between us and pulled me in for another hug. I felt his chin rest on top of my head, felt his deep breath. I had no idea such an intense man would be one to coddle. It felt good to be held, to be offered reassurance and comfort from the simple gesture.

"You are *not* frigid," he replied. "You're spirited and fiery and that kiss... it didn't feel cold to me."

That's true, it was anything but cold.

"Go peek and see what's happening in the other room," Sully said. He squeezed me once, then let me go.

Taking a deep breath, I went to the peephole. I knew it looked into the small room beside the parlor, brightened by lamps and plenty of red velvet to make it bold. Comfortably lying on his back on the settee was a man; one knee was bent and a foot rested on the floor beside a woman's rumpled drawers. I couldn't see his face because Amelia was sitting atop it. Right on top of it! Her breasts were lifted out of her corset so her nipples were exposed. Her head was back, her eyes closed and her lips parted as the man put his mouth on her... there. He gripped her hips and held her in place so he could lick her pussy.

I gasped. This was not something I'd seen before.

"I'd like to do that to you," Parker murmured. He stood directly behind me—I hadn't heard him approach—and I startled, pulling my eye away from the hole. With his palms on either side of my head, I wasn't going anywhere. Against my lower back I felt his cock, hard and thick.

"Keep watching. I want you to sit on my face just like that so

I can eat your pussy. I want to know your taste, swallow down every bit of your cream. I want to make you scream your pleasure."

My pussy ached as I watched the carnal sight. The man was proficient at his task, for while he held her hips securely with his hands, she undulated on top of him, crying out with abandon.

"I'll push down your corset so I can suck one plump nipple into my mouth, then the other as Parker uses his tongue on your little clit." Sully came to the side of me and whispered in my other ear.

They spoke as I continued to watch as the man shifted Amelia forward, her hands grabbing onto the back of the settee for support, her thighs quivering. Chloe had said she sometimes pretended to enjoy herself; Amelia definitely wasn't acting.

"Your cheeks are flushed, your breath is quick. You want us to touch you like that," Parker said.

A hand stroked down my back. I wasn't sure whose hand it was, but it changed the experience of watching a couple in such a carnal union. I could *feel* what I was seeing, too. A hand tugged at my long dress, up and up it went until I felt fingers graze my stocking, then play with the edge of it, just touching my bare thigh.

I gasped, not only from the touch, but because the woman screamed her pleasure then. My pussy ached for its own fulfillment.

The door to the kitchen swung open and the hem of my dress fell to the floor. Sully turned and faced the person, shielding me. Parker retreated. Panicked, I spun about, my back pressed against the wall and glanced up at Parker. I felt like a child eating a slice of birthday cake before the party. Instead of scolding, he smiled at me, then winked. How just a smile eased my tension, I had no idea.

The person must have realized they'd interrupted something, for their footsteps retreated.

"Perhaps we shouldn't fuck you on the table with a bowl of cabbage beside you," Parker commented. "Shall we go upstairs instead?"

Sully turned so I was once again between the two of them, a spot they seemed to enjoy placing me. I couldn't deny my eagerness. I could only nod as the feelings coursing through me could only be alleviated by these men.

6

ARKER

Closing the door behind me, I turned the lock and faced our skittish bride.

"When we are in the bedroom, the first task for you is to strip. Tonight, you get a reprieve."

When Mary's eyes widened, and then her mouth opened to respond, I raised my hand to keep her quiet.

"You are not yet ready and more important, we want to undress you ourselves."

"That's right. You're like a Christmas present in August," Sully said, circling Mary as if she were prey. It was only a matter of time before he ate her up. "I'm looking forward to finding out what's underneath the wrapping."

The room was appointed with a large four-poster bed, quite elaborate for a brothel. There was a plush chair in the corner with a velvet-topped ottoman before it. The one window had brocade curtains, but the glass was shielded by a second set of curtains, these closed. Everything was a deep red. Decadent and exotic.

I also knew why Miss Rose offered this room. It was not one of the girls' private rooms on loan. It was for special guests who paid well to spend the night in such decadence. It was also for special guests who liked their women tied to the bedposts or positioned on all fours on the ottoman for either a spanking or double fucking. Perhaps both. I would have to thank Miss Rose in the morning.

"Are there peepholes into this room?" Sully asked Mary.

She looked around, but shrugged. "I don't know. I've never been in here before."

Sully came up behind her, slid his hands around her waist and moved them up so they cupped her full breasts. "Someone could be watching us right now? Seeing my hands on you?"

She stiffened and tried to pull away, but her action only pushed her breasts more fully into his cupped hands.

"Shh," he whispered. "They'll see a beautiful woman with her men."

He held her still a minute longer, letting her know who was in charge.

Moving his hands up to the top of her dress, he began undoing the buttons down the front, one by one. "*We* want to see you."

I sat on the bed, watched as her delicate collarbones appeared, the upper swells of her breasts, the fine corset. Sully was swift and efficient, working the sleeves off her arms, then pushing the heavy fabric of her dress over her hips and into a puddle on the floor.

A sigh escaped my lips. "You're not any less dressed than before," I muttered, displeased with the layers upon layers of underthings Mary wore.

"This is what a woman always wears," she countered, looking down at herself.

Sully undid the ties on her petticoat, pushed that down to fall on top of her dress. Then her drawers.

Her corset and shift remained.

Reaching around, Sully worked the stays of her corset loose, then tossed it aside.

Mary took a deep breath, released it. It was so snug, surely her tender skin was marked. All that remained was her shift.

My fingers itched to touch her, but I restrained myself. "When we dress you in the morning, all you get is your shift beneath your dress. Nothing else."

She looked more appalled at the idea of missing some undergarments beneath her clothes than the fact that she was standing before us in only a shift. My words did distract her from the fact that her breasts pressed tautly against the sheer shift and her rosy nipples were pebbled and clearly defined. The material was so delicate I could even see the dark hair that shielded her pussy.

"I can't go without a corset!" she replied, her voice rising.

Sully cupped her breasts in his palms. They were large for her small frame, a good handful. "Mmm," he murmured. "You offer such delectable bounty. A looser one then, that doesn't mar this pretty flesh."

I was glad Sully had the same thoughts. Mary's breasts were heavy teardrops and would be uncomfortable if left unbound, but she still needed to be able to breathe.

Sully continued to play and I watched as her eyes changed

from aware to aroused, her head falling back to rest against his shoulder. It was uncomfortable to sit, my cock hard and long, pressing against my pants. Opening the front placket, I pulled it free and I began to stroke it.

Once she was well and truly lost to the feelings of Sully's hands on her, he was able to lift the thin garment that separated her delectable body from our sight and toss it, too, onto the floor.

I groaned then, seeing her completely bare. Stunningly beautiful, and she was all ours.

Her nipples were a soft pink, hard and pointed straight toward me. Her waist was narrow and her hips flared out, wide and full. She was not a waif, all skin and bones, but lushly built. Her legs were long and shapely. Between them....

I groaned again at the sight of that dark thatch of curls, the pink lips that peeked out from beneath.

"Let's see what you learned from your visits," I said, continuing to stroke myself. "What's this?"

I hoped her arousal would lessen her inhibitions and I was right. "Your cock."

Sully's hands gently stroked her. Up her sides, across her belly, along the outside of her thighs.

"And this?" Sully cupped her center.

"My... my pussy."

"That's right. Let's see if I can make you purr," he murmured into her ear as he worked his fingers into her. Soon enough, she was riding them, wild and eager for her release. She had no inhibitions and was very sensitive, quick to respond, quick to arousal.

"What do you want?" Sully murmured, hand buried between her thighs.

I liked the look of it, his dark hand, all work-worn and large, parting her creamy, lush thighs.

"I want to come. Make me come," she demanded.

"Have you ever come before?" Sully asked.

She nodded, bit her lip.

"With your own fingers?" he added.

"Yes, but it's not... it's not like this."

I smiled then, as her voice shifted from aroused to desperate. "No, it's better with your men. You'll have to show us how you touch yourself. Later."

"Now," she commanded. "Make me come now."

Pulling his fingers free, Sully lightly spanked her pussy. She gasped and her eyes flared open.

I shook my head. "You don't tell us what to do, sweetheart. You may have watched other couples fuck. You may have even touched yourself and found your pleasure, but we control it now."

"We say how," Sully said, spanking her once more between her parted thighs. Her lips there were swollen and red, her clit poking out and so responsive. "We say when."

Amazingly, when Sully spanked her clit again, she came, her body shuddering and a groan escaped. Her body slumped in his hold and he wrapped a hand about her waist to keep her upright. We shared a telling look, then Sully spanked her pussy once more as she writhed in his hold, then plunged his fingers inside her.

"Yes!" she cried, lost to the pleasure, coming up onto her toes.

Holy fuck, Mary liked it when she had her pussy spanked. She came without a cock inside her. She came because we told her we controlled her now.

"I feel her maidenhead," Sully said, pulling his fingers from her and putting them to Mary's lips. "Open."

She did as he commanded and Sully slipped his two dripping fingers into her mouth.

"Taste yourself. You are a little whore," he murmured in her ear. "Coming without our permission. Coming because of your pussy getting spanked. We haven't even gotten our cocks in you and you're so greedy."

"Isn't that right, sweetheart?" I asked, stroking my cock again. Shit, the sight of her, so lost in pleasure, made me desperate to get inside her. "You're *our* little whore. Just for me and Sully."

"Perhaps we will show you off to others, but not yet. We, too, are greedy."

She was panting now, her breasts rising and falling, her nipples softening before my eyes as her body was finally sated. But we were not done. We were *far* from done.

"You came without permission, therefore you will be punished."

A little whimper escaped her throat. She didn't fear the word *punished*, only clenched Sully's forearm.

Turning her about, he pointed to the ottoman. "Hands and knees, Mary. You were so beautiful when you came, but you didn't obey us. Now we're going to spank your ass a nice shade of pink."

"But... but it was just too good!" she argued, but walked to the cushioned piece of furniture, ideal for a punishment spanking.

"If you like having your pussy spanked, then you're going to love this," Sully added.

As she moved into position with her ass up, her breasts

swaying beneath her, I said, "If she loves it, it's not a punishment."

I stroked over her lush curves, slid a hand down the inside of one thigh. While I encountered her copious arousal, I spread her knees further apart. "Down on your forearms."

When she complied, her nipples touched the cool leather and her ass thrust upwards. Her pussy, so pink and wet and perfect, was on complete display. My cock ached to plunge inside, my balls pulling up tight to my body, but I would wait. For now. For now, I would enjoy this first time with Mary, learning what she liked, what she loved, what made her pussy flood.

And so I brought my hand down on her ass, the spot turning instantly red. She gasped at the surprise of it, then the sound shifted to a whimper as the sting of it surely settled and morphed into heat.

"We may have to think of something that isn't quite so... pleasant."

She cried out and came back up onto her hands, her head lifting so she looked at Sully.

He shook his head, and told her to return to her position. His voice was deep and commanding and she obeyed instantly.

I spanked her again, but in another spot, then another. While Mary wiggled her hips, she didn't shift out of position. With each spank, she moaned, the sound wrapping around my balls and squeezing tight.

Sully squatted down directly before her, cupped her chin. He kissed her gently. "You like being spanked by your men, don't you?"

Her face was flushed, her skin damp. Her hair, pinned in a

tight bun at her nape, came loose in long tendrils and clung to her cheeks and neck.

She looked at him, their faces close. "Oh yes. It... it hurts, but then it doesn't. My skin is hot and tight and... I want to come."

Sully smiled at Mary's admission. "That's a good girl for telling the truth. While you could have told us differently, your body doesn't lie. But remember, this is supposed to be a punishment and you're not supposed to like it."

"I can't... not like it," she admitted.

Sully stood to his full height and came to stand beside me. We took a moment to just look our fill, at our virgin wife, naked and on her hands and knees, reddened ass thrust high, her pussy swollen and weeping with need. She was gorgeous... and ours.

"While she's a virgin, she's definitely not innocent," I told Sully. "Perhaps we can begin our training now."

Turning her head, she looked over her shoulder at us. Her hair was wild about her. "Training?"

I pointed to my cock. "You'll take this, sweetheart. In your pussy, your mouth and your ass."

Sully undid his pants, pulled his cock free, and her eyes widened. "And you'll take mine, too. At the same time."

Her mouth fell open as she glanced back and forth at our two eager cocks. Yes, we'd just surprised her. Sully chuckled. "Didn't know about that, did you?"

She shook her head and licked her lips. As I went to retrieve the glass jar of ointment from the dresser, I could only imagine what was going through her pretty head.

7

ARY

It felt *so* good. How did something that was painful feel so good? When Parker's palm connected with my bottom, it hurt! That sharp, stinging pain that seeped into me and made me cry out. But at the same time, my pussy clenched and ached to be filled with his cock. I'd seen it and it was big and thick and so terribly hard. Bigger than any other cock I'd seen. The men I'd seen while eavesdropping were small in comparison. And now, because he was spanking me, I wanted him to fuck me.

What did that make me? Oh God. Did that mean I'd like—

"Where did that pretty head of yours go?" Sully asked, stroking down my back. "Something's made you tense all of a sudden."

"I was just thinking."

"Mmm," Parker murmured. "Perhaps I wasn't spanking you

hard enough to forget everything else?"

I stiffened again.

"Mary," Sully scolded. "Out with it."

"I thought of Benson. If I like it when you spank me, if I like the pain you bring, would I like what he'd do to me after all?"

Both men came around to kneel before me. Sully tugged me up so I knelt on the ottoman before them.

"Benson likes to hurt women. That's what brings him pleasure. Inflicting it, the marks, her response. He likes to see her hurt."

Parker nodded at Sully's words. "We would never truly hurt you. You liked your spanking and that's why we gave it to you. We are the ones in control. We get pleasure from dominating you, when you submit to our commands. While you might feel pain, it's mild and it brings immediate pleasure."

I thought about his words. When Parker spanked me, it had hurt, but not terribly and pleasure morphed from it almost immediately. I'd liked it. No, I'd *loved* it.

"Does the idea of being whipped appeal to you?" Sully asked.

My eyes widened and I crossed my arms over my chest. I shook my head vehemently.

Parker smiled and they each took one of my hands in theirs. Their thumbs stroked over my palms, the gesture gentle and soothing.

"That's the difference, sweetheart," Parker added. "You don't want it and so we won't do it. It's not what makes you happy, what brings you pleasure, so it doesn't make us happy or bring us pleasure either."

"You like spanking me?"

They grinned wickedly, glanced down at their cocks, both jutting thickly from between their legs.

"Enough about Benson. We're not done with you yet. You need to be punished still for coming without permission. Clearly a simple spanking is *not* punishment."

Sully touched the tip of my nose. "Yes?" he asked.

Even though they were so commanding, so dominant, they ensured that I was all right.

I nodded once. "Yes," I whispered.

"Back into position, sweetheart." Parker's voice lost that tenderness and was deep and commanding. The tone sent a chill down my spine and I obeyed.

"It is my turn then," Sully said, moving around behind me. "Perhaps Parker is just too nice."

I laughed at that, but it turned into a moan when his blunt finger slid through my folds, then slipped inside me.

I moaned at the feel of something inside my pussy. It burned a little, for his finger was big and I *was* a virgin.

"Dripping," he said before pulling his finger out.

I felt empty. Wiggling my hips, I hoped he'd take my hint and put his finger back in.

A hand came down on my bottom. Not harder than before, just... different. "We say how and when, sweetheart. You want my finger back?"

"Oh yes," I moaned. I wanted to clench down on it, pull it into me.

When it returned, it wasn't where I expected. The slick tip pressed against the darkest of places. I stiffened, but a hand settled on my bottom as the finger swirled about.

"By your response to Sully's finger pressing against your tight asshole, we can assume you never saw a woman get her ass fucked?" Parker asked.

I shook my head, focusing on the odd sensations Sully's finger wrought. He wasn't rough, but gentle and yet insistent. I dropped my head between my hands, my forehead resting on the cool leather. I glanced through my parted thighs and saw Sully's strong legs.

The finger retreated, and I sighed, but then it returned, slick and cold. This time, his pressure was more insistent, but still gentle, pressing and opening me.

I gasped as he slowly pushed into me.

"Relax. Let me in. Good girl. Another deep breath. Yes, like that. See? Your ass opened right up for me."

My fingers clawed at the leather ottoman as Sully gained entrance. I was stretched and the tip of his finger filled me. It didn't hurt, but was uncomfortable.

"Why? Why would you want to—"

Wondering why they'd think I'd want a finger inserted there, I began to ask them just that, but instead of a verbal response, Sully pulled his finger back just a touch and where his finger stroked, it came alive. A tingling flare of heat had me crying out, and quite loudly.

Sully chuckled, then worked his finger back in. Since I was eager for it, I was relaxed and he slipped a touch deeper than before, only to retreat.

"Yes!" I cried. "Oh dear lord, yes."

Sweat broke out across my skin and my need to come went from a warmth to a raging fire throughout my body.

"This is just the tip of my finger fucking your ass,

sweetheart. Imagine if it were my cock," Sully said, slowly moving his finger in and out.

"I'm going to come," I warned. It was like a steam train, unable to stop.

"Oh no," Parker warned. "Your punishment is to hold off your pleasure. You are not allowed to come. Sully's going to spank you ten times and you'll count each one."

His hand came down and I heard the loud crack before I felt the burn of it. But that didn't register in my mind as much as his finger in my ass slid in even deeper. I moaned, so woefully and desperately. How did it feel so good?

"Count, Mary," Sully said.

"One," I breathed, rubbing my heated cheek against the leather.

Spank!

Sully's finger pulled almost out of my ass and I saw colorful lights behind my eyelids.

"Two!"

Spank!

His finger slid in even deeper.

Spank after spank, I counted. Spank after spank, Sully worked his finger in and out of my ass.

My body was desperate to come. The need to let go, to give over to the sheer bliss of it, was my every thought. It was a painful pleasure. Sweet pain that made my nipples harden, my clit ache. *Don't come. Don't come. Don't come.*

I counted and willed my need back, just enough so that when I whimpered, "Ten," I was on the very brink.

Sully pulled his finger completely from me.

"No! Please, no," I cried. I didn't want his finger to stop.

Their Stolen Bride

With an arm about my waist, Sully lifted me into his arms as I watched Parker lie down on the large ottoman, his head and back resting comfortably, his legs extended off and his knees bent so his feet rested on the floor. His cock jutted straight toward the ceiling, clear fluid beading at the narrow slit.

Sully lowered me so my knees were on either side of Parker's waist, my pussy hovering directly over his cock.

"Time to give yourself to us," Parker said, his cock in hand. He stroked himself, the flesh red and swollen and angry looking. "Ever seen a woman ride a man's cock?"

I nodded, biting my lip.

"Settle yourself down on Parker's cock," Sully ordered. "Take him nice and deep."

Bending my knees, I felt the flared head nudge my pussy and slip over my slick folds. I shifted, then settled, as his cock nudged my entrance.

"He's so big," I murmured, feeling pussy lips part. My ass tingled from Sully's finger and my body so desperate to come. The idea of this large cock filling me, tearing my maidenhead wasn't even scary.

"I am, sweetheart. I'm going to fill you right up," Parker grinned.

I pressed down on him and he slid in one delectable inch at a time. He was stretching me, filling me and I gasped.

"Ah, there it is, the last barrier between us," he growled.

I winced at the sharp bite of pain as his cock nudged that thin membrane.

"It's time to make you mine. Ours."

Sully came up behind me, put a hand gently on my shoulder as I felt his slick finger once again at my ass. The combination of the cock halfway inside me, teasing me and Sully's finger had me shaking.

"When we fill you up, you have permission to come," Sully murmured. I saw Parker glance over my shoulder at Sully.

Putting his hands on my hips, Parker thrust up as he pulled me down. At the same time, Sully's slick finger slid up and into my ass.

The pain of Parker's cock breaking my maidenhead, his cock opening my pussy up, the heated sting of my bottom and Sully's finger deep in my ass coalesced into this swirl of painful pleasure so brilliantly bright that I saw white behind my eyelids. I came then, my back bowed and my head tossed back, my scream of pleasure escaping. I couldn't hold it back. I couldn't hold anything back. I writhed and shifted, panted and cried as I came.

Nothing, *nothing* prepared me for how this felt. I was lost, tossed into the wind and battered. I couldn't control it, couldn't hold on to anything, but I knew I was safe. The feel of Parker's hands gripping my hips and Sully's hand on my shoulder were my anchors, holding me in place and allowing me to let go while I knew they'd catch me. They'd keep me safe.

Slowly, I returned to myself. The men had held themselves still as I came, Parker's cock throbbing and pulsing inside me, Sully's finger insistent and deep.

Opening my eyes, I looked down at Parker. His cheeks were flushed, his neck muscles corded.

"That, sweetheart, is punishment."

A wicked grin spread across his face and I couldn't help but smile.

"You'll be punished when you disobey, but we promise that you'll be rewarded after."

I fell onto his chest, the fabric of his shirt scratchy against my sensitive nipples. "I'm so tired," I murmured.

"Oh no, you don't." With gentle hands, he pushed me back up so I sat astride again, his cock shifting within.

"It's Parker's turn, Mary," Sully said. "Take his cock for a ride."

Sully's finger was still inside me and I clenched down. Both men groaned. I felt powerful in that moment. Sated, sweaty and wonderfully powerful.

Glancing over my shoulder, I looked at Sully. "But… but your finger."

He lifted his eyebrows and smiled wickedly. "Get used to having something fill your ass."

What did he mean by that exactly?

"But—"

"Do we know what's best for you?" he asked.

"Yes, but… something there, often?"

He pulled his finger back slightly, then pumped it into me, his other fingers bumping against my spanked bottom.

"Yes." That's all he said about the matter. "Fuck Parker's cock."

I wanted to move, my pussy eager, so I pushed off my knees and raised up. Parker's cock slid over my inner walls and made me gasp. At the same time, I came up off of Sully's finger, but not completely. I was still open for him, too.

Lowering myself, I felt them go deep.

I tossed my head back as the pleasure returned. No pain, no discomfort from the loss of my virginity. I didn't know how I could want more pleasure after my first orgasm, but my body was warm and limber and ready all over again. My clit rubbed against Parker's lower belly and I shifted, squirming with having both my holes filled.

"Let go and enjoy. Come whenever you want."

At Sully's permission, I began to move. I remembered seeing the whores fucking men like this and I knew now why they enjoyed it so much. But none of them ever had a second man put a finger deep inside her ass so she was fucking herself in both holes. It was dark and carnal and wrong, and yet it felt wonderful.

Sully and Parker did not think less of me for my wanton display. In fact, they pushed me into it, pushed me to discover and enjoy the most deviant of desires.

That was all forgotten as instinct and a drive to another orgasm took over. I lifted and lowered, fucked myself on Parker's cock. His fingers clenched my hips, but he let me move as I needed. Sully's finger was insistent and went so deep each time, the sensations it brought about as I raised and lowered myself over the bumpy digit pushed me over the edge.

I came again, clenching down, my inner walls rippling and pulsing.

As I came, my hips stopped moving and I succumbed. Parker took over then, lifting and lowering me as his hips thrust up, his turn to use me for his own pleasure. His breath came in deep pants, his pace uneven as his need took over. I felt him swell and thicken inside of me before he thrust so deep I felt him bump my womb. As he came, he groaned. I came then, a gentle, rolling pleasure at the feel of his hot seed pulsing into me.

This time, when I fell forward onto his chest, he wrapped his arms about me, stroked my slick back.

As Parker caught his breath, as I lay limp and replete, Sully

Their Stolen Bride

gently slipped his finger free and I whimpered. I heard him shuck his clothes and saw them fall to the floor beside me.

The flesh on flesh stroking sound had me turn my head slightly and I watched as a naked Sully stroked his very eager cock.

"Sully's turn, sweetheart," Parker murmured. "Look at that cock. He needs you. He needs your pussy."

Parker gripped me as he sat up, then shifted and placed me on my back just as he'd been.

Standing, he put his spent cock back in his pants.

Sully stepped up to the edge of the ottoman, took hold of my ankles and slid me down the length of it so my bottom was at the edge. The sore skin tingled against the cool leather.

While intense, Sully had always been gentle with me. Even his finger had probed my ass in an almost delicate way. But now, now he was keeping his inner beast at bay with the thinnest of threads. His body was coated in a sheen of sweat. His face was flushed, his lips a thin line. The veins in his temple pulsed and his cock dripped fluid onto the wood floor.

Seeing him this way had me eager. I'd made him this way. While the judge had been afraid of Sully, I was the one who reduced the outlaw to his basest of beings.

"Pull your knees back. Wider. Hold them like that."

I positioned myself as Sully commanded. I liked the sharp bite of his voice, doing as he wanted. I knew now that while he would do what he wished with me, I'd come, too. I was sure of it.

Placing one knee on the floor, then the other, he knelt between my spread thighs. He was at the perfect height to have his cock lined up with my pussy. Without any preamble, he pushed right in on one long stroke. He went deeper than

Parker, if that were even possible. Perhaps it was the angle, perhaps it was because his cock was longer, but I felt every thick inch.

He took me hard, his need was that great. Eyes on my pussy, he watched as his cock disappeared inside me and came back out coated in a mixture of my arousal and Parker's seed.

"We're one now, Mary. Your pussy, Parker's seed, my cock. I'm going to fill you up, too. Our seed's going to drip from you all night, make you all nice and wet to take you again."

He told me what he was going to do, how he was going to fuck me, how Parker was going to take me as he plunged into me.

Parker knelt beside the ottoman and cupped my breasts, played with them, tugged on the nipples as Sully didn't stop. I bowed my back and held onto my knees as Sully came, pushing me into one last orgasm. Like Parker, I felt his seed fill me, felt the hot spurts coat my pussy. I was marked by both of them and I loved that almost Neanderthal concept.

Our deep breaths were all we could hear; the scent of fucking, thick and pungent, filled the air. I was a sweaty, sticky mess and felt sore and used and... well fucked.

As Sully pulled out, I felt their combined seed start to trickle from me.

Sully's hand cupped my pussy. "That's a gorgeous sight, sweetheart. Your pussy, all swollen and well used, our seed dripping from it."

Parker's fingers joined Sully's, rubbing their seed over me, working it back into me. "We don't want you to lose a drop."

Parker smiled at me as their hands moved over my most intimate of places. "And you thought you weren't ready."

8

ARY

I soaked in a tub filled with steaming water in the washroom, eyes closed. The scent of rose came from the bars of soap and oils tucked into a copper basket hooked on the side of the copper tub. Copper. Most likely pulled from my father's mine.

The brothel was quiet this early in the morning; all the patrons had been satisfied and sent on their way, all the women sleeping off their night of work. It was the perfect time to ease all of my new aches and pains. Not pains, but I was definitely sore. I couldn't help the grin that stretched across my face remembering exactly how I got that way.

"It was that good?"

I opened my eyes to see Chloe standing in the doorway. She wore just a simple white shift and a shawl about her shoulders. She grinned at me and waggled her eyebrows.

"It was... better than good." I tried to think of an appropriate adjective, but there was none. I doubted my childhood tutor could think of a word appropriate for how a woman feels after being fucked by two men.

Chloe came in and closed the door behind her, careful to let the door latch as quietly as possible.

"I am amazed your men let you out from beneath them."

I grabbed a bar of soap, played with it, let it slip through my fingers. "They stirred, of course."

"Of course," she giggled, moving to sit on a short stool, her knees tucked up to her chest. Her red hair was plaited into a thick braid that fell over her shoulder, a simple blue ribbon at the bottom.

"But they understood my interest in a bath."

"I bet they did. You have all the luck. Not one beautiful cowboy, but two. And Shooter Sullivan, in bed." She sighed then. "I bet his weapon is *mighty* powerful."

I rolled my eyes at her innuendo.

"That other man, Benson? I have more reason why you shouldn't have married him."

At the mention of his name, I shifted, the water sloshing toward the edge of the tub. "Oh?"

"One of my men last night is his foreman." Chloe walked over to the tub, leaned forward and put her hand by her mouth as if to tell me a secret. "The mine, there's no copper. The vein's run dry."

My eyes widened. "Dry?"

I couldn't believe it. The man spent money as if it came from a well and he just pumped it up out of the ground. If his mine was dry, he certainly wasn't behaving as if he were in trouble.

She bit her lip, then nodded. "Enough about that little shit. Tell me everything about last night."

I poked a bubble on the water's surface. "What?"

"Mary Millard," she started, then giggled again. "I mean, Mary Sullivan, you were a virgin last night and your first time was with *two* men. I've never even been with two men and I'm a two-bit whore in Butte."

I narrowed my eyes at her. "You are much more than a two-bit whore," I admonished.

"And as I said before, I've never been with two men." She leaned forward, full of eagerness on her flushed cheeks. "I want to know all the details."

"I don't know what to tell you, for I have no other experience for comparison."

Chloe was contemplative. "True. Then I shall ask you questions that you must answer."

I wasn't sure how much I wanted to share. It was one thing for me to peek into other people's sexual escapades, another for me to delve into mine, even as minimal as they were.

"First of all, you are no longer a virgin, correct?"

"That's correct." That was a safe question. I'd married two dominant, virile men. There wasn't a chance I was making it through my wedding night without it being consummated.

"Did they both fuck you?"

I could see my breasts beneath the water, my nipples soft, but I remembered how hard they were when Parker took one, then the other, in his mouth.

"Yes."

"Together?" Her question was full of amazement.

I shook my head. I'd piled my hair up on top of my head

with a few pins, but the curls swung about my face and neck. "They said I wasn't ready, that I needed to be trained."

"Mmm," she replied thoughtfully.

"Chloe." I had a question for her, but was afraid to ask. But I took a deep breath, for perhaps she was the *only* person I could ask. "In this context, what does it mean to be trained?"

She pushed her legs out straight in front of her. "Your men are thoughtful lovers. They want to fuck your ass, but it's probably really tight."

I flicked my gaze at her, then looked away. I offered a sheepish nod, for this discussion about such a private part of my body made me horribly uncomfortable, but I wanted her to continue.

"Your ass—not you—needs to be trained, to be slowly stretched so that it can take a cock without hurting you."

"Oh." I thought of Sully's finger and how he'd used that to *train* me.

"How would they go about doing that?" I asked, not letting on about Sully's finger. *That* I wasn't sharing.

"Oh, well, with plugs."

I frowned, thinking about the one at the bottom of the tub.

She stood, then went right for the door. "Be right back!"

She was gone before I could even wonder where she went. I used the soap on my body, then cupped my hands to rinse my shoulders. I was finishing when Chloe returned, closing the door once again behind her. She held up a small object.

"This is a plug." She waggled her eyebrows.

It looked like a... "It's a sock darner?"

She shook her head and giggled again. "No, silly. It goes up your ass. See how it's narrow at the top and then flares out?

That stretches you open, then it narrows again. This here is the part that sticks out and holds it in place."

"Is that yours?"

She looked at me as if I were not right in the head. "Of course not. We have a carpenter make these for the brothel. This was in the box of ones just delivered."

My mouth fell open at the very idea and my bottom clenched at the thought of that being put inside me. "I've never... I mean, no one ever used one of those when we were watching."

She put her finger to her lip. "I don't remember watching with you anyone getting ass fucked, or even playing. If we did, they wouldn't have used one of these because they would have been experienced and wouldn't have needed any help."

That made sense.

"Then—" I was about to ask her another question, but a knock disrupted me.

"Mary."

Chloe looked to me.

"It's Sully."

"Do you want me to let him in?" she whispered.

"As if anything's going to keep him out?" I responded.

Chloe opened the door and Sully stepped inside. Dressed once again, his shirt was untucked and his feet were bare. With his dark hair mussed and whiskers on his jaw, he looked rugged and very handsome.

When he saw me in the tub, his eyes narrowed and heated. From his height, he could see all of me. I might have been a virgin the night before, but I knew that look. "I came to check on you."

"Chloe and I were just chatting."

"What's that?" he asked, pointing to the plug in Chloe's hand.

Her eyes widened and looked to me, slightly panicked. I appreciated her worries for me, for what we'd talked about had been in confidence. Now our conversation was secret no longer.

"It's... it's an ass plug," she murmured.

"Is it yours?" he asked.

Chloe shook her head, but didn't give him the funny look she'd given me when I asked the same question. She seemed a little afraid of Sully, or at least of Shooter Sullivan. "No, it's from the carpenter's delivery box."

"Ah, good. Excellent timing then. May I have it?"

After a quick glance at me, she handed it over. It seemed so small in Sully's big hand, but I could only imagine it fitting inside *me*.

"All done?" he asked me.

I nodded, for the water was getting cold and the room crowded.

Looking about, he took a bath sheet from a hook on the wall and came over to me. I stood, water dripping. It was strange being naked with him, but after last night, it was silly to be embarrassed. Sully offered me a hand and I stepped out, then wrapped the sheet about me.

As he did, he said, "Parker is awake and we should leave before it becomes too late. But first, we will shave your pussy. Now that we have this gift from Chloe, we will begin your ass training, too."

My mouth fell open as I held the snuggly sheet about me. "I beg your pardon?" I asked. He said shaved?

He went to a glass-fronted cabinet and opened the door, found some shaving supplies, then turned about.

"Shave?" I squeaked.

I glanced at Chloe, who only bit her lower lip. "I'll... um, I'll leave you two, or three—" she giggled again, "—alone for now, and say goodbye later."

She slipped from the door and I was alone with Sully.

"Shave?" I repeated.

His hands were full with a straight razor, a short strap of leather to sharpen it and a shaving cup, an ivory-handled brush sticking out the top. Plus, the plug. Oh my.

"Yes, we're going to shave your pussy bare."

I frowned. "But why?"

He went to the door, opened it, peeked out into the hall then glanced back at me. He had a dark glint to his eye and the corner of his mouth tipped up. "Because I want to eat that sweet pussy and I want it nice and smooth."

"Eat?"

"Come. Parker is waiting. After your shave, we can acquaint your tight little ass with this very nice plug."

"I don't want to be shaved," I admitted. "And that... that plug won't fit inside of me."

He took my elbow and tugged me down the hall and into our room. He used his hip to close the door behind him.

Parker sat on the side of the bed and was pulling on a boot. He took in the sight of me in just a bath sheet.

He stood, came over to me and kissed me. As soon as his mouth met mine, every thought was forgotten. His soft lips brushed over mine, once, twice. Then he took it deeper, his tongue tangling with mine. His hands gripped my upper arms and I felt warm all over, this time not from the bathwater. My pussy clenched in memory of what a kiss led to.

When Parker finally lifted his head, I discovered the bath

sheet was in a puddle at my feet and I was completely bare to them.

"She doesn't want to be shaved," Sully said.

Parker arched a brow. "Oh? Why not?"

The answer was simple to me.

"Why would I?" I replied.

He grinned then, just before he picked me up and laid me on the bed. He stood at the side and with hands on my thighs, tugged me to the very edge. He placed one of my feet on the soft blanket, then the other before kneeling down. Pushing up on my elbows, I looked down my bare body at him. His head was directly in line with my pussy.

He lowered his head then, putting his mouth on me. There!

"Oh my," I gasped.

The tip of his tongue moved along my seam, then, with his hands on my inner thighs, used his thumbs to spread my lower lips apart. With more intent than gentleness, he licked me. Over my clit, over each fold, then at my entrance.

I raised my hips so he could do that some more, but he lifted his head and grinned. Using the back of his hand, he wiped his mouth, which was slick with... oh. He was slick with my arousal.

"This is why we want you shaved." Parker held up his hand and Sully handed him the shaving brush. "Just wait. You'll see. Trust us that you will like it. Love it, in fact."

"But all of it?" I wondered. Did it all have to go away?

Parker had a thoughtful look as he lightly tugged at my short curls. "I'll leave a little bit right here. A little pale triangle that points right to my—"

"Our," Sully corrected.

"Our perfect pussy."

I wasn't sure if I should be thankful or not.

"Chloe gave us this, too." Sully held the plug out for Parker to take and I blushed furiously.

"Sully," I whimpered.

After placing the shaving cup on the bed beside my thigh, Parker took it, then studied it. From this close, I could see that it was a dark wood, honed smooth. It *was* big, but it wasn't too much larger than Sully's finger.

With the lightest of touches, Parker brushed over my clit, then slid lower, then lower and even lower still to my back entrance. His finger swirled and pressed lightly against me. "Once you're shaved we'll put this plug in here. Start your training. You want to take us both, don't you, sweetheart? One in that hot little pussy and one in your virgin ass."

"Sit still for Parker, Mary, and when he's done, when that pussy's bare and that ass is filled, we'll let you come," Sully promised. "You get to decide if it's with Parker's mouth or my cock."

Oh my.

9

ULLY

Leaving the brothel, when there was a perfectly good bed and a very sated bride, was a hard task. Miss Rose had horses, ready and waiting for us to take to Bridgewater. We'd ridden out with some simple provisions, but it was only a few hours to Bridgewater and we made it—without any issue—by lunchtime. Of course, thinking of Mary's pussy with a little patch of blond hair, my seed trickling from it, and the dark base of the ass plug parting her cheeks had me hard the entire way. It was an uncomfortable way to travel. I wanted to take Mary right to our home and keep her naked and in bed for at least a week to assuage the need I had for her, but we had to assume Benson would not relent where Mary was concerned.

He did not know more than my last name, so it would take time, even with ample money to put at the task, to find me.

Therefore, we had some time, a few days at least, but we would not risk our friends. They needed to know what was most likely coming so the women and children were safe and a plan was in place to end Benson once and for all.

Because of this, we veered from our own house and went right to Ian and Kane's, where those who were not working met for meals. While there were some surprised faces as we introduced Mary as our bride, everyone was pleased. She'd been whisked into the kitchens with the ladies, and Mason, who was helping with the cooking. At the mention of Mary being a Millard, we'd settled into Kane's office with the door closed. None of us were afraid of Benson, but he was a real threat.

"He wants Mary," I said to the group. Besides Parker and Kane, Andrew, Robert and Brody joined us. While not faring from the same country, we were all experienced military men. One rich asshole was an annoyance that had to be dealt with.

"That means he wants you gone," Kane said. "And I don't mean run out of the Territory."

His English accent clipped his words. He, along with Ian, was the first to marry. Emma was their wife and they had a baby girl, Ellie.

Kane and Ian, along with a few others in the British military, started Bridgewater. A commanding officer of theirs had murdered a woman and framed Ian with the terrible deed. Instead of facing the social and political injustices of an English trial—it was a Scot's word against a titled Brit—they fled to America for a simple life.

That was exactly what I wanted. A simple life, but then I married Mary.

"If you're dead, he can marry her and join his mine with her father's," Kane continued. "Or whatever the hell their plan is."

"Money. It's the basis for it, definitely." Parker crossed his arms. "He doesn't know about me, or at least he doesn't know she's mine, too."

I leaned against the wall and stared at the other men. "That means that if I die, Parker will legally make her his," I said.

"Reggie Benson's a mean son of a bitch," Robert said. He was leaning on the edge of the desk and his fingers stroked over his beard. "I haven't met him, but his name precedes him."

Andrew shook his head. "That mine accident last year, it was preventable, but he didn't give a shit."

There'd been a collapse, for Benson didn't provide enough lumber to shore up the walls. There'd been a cave-in and four miners had died. Within a day, he had five replacements. Those were just like the men who'd been on the train with us, eager for a new start. To Benson, they were expendable.

"You have what he wants," Andrew added. "He's going to come after you on principle alone."

Kane shook his head, steepled his fingers as he leaned back in his desk chair. "He won't come himself. He'll send men. A man like him wouldn't get his hands dirty."

I pushed off the wall. "He's coming after Mary's husband, not me specifically. He doesn't know who he's dealing with."

Parker laughed. "That's right. He has no idea he's up against Shooter Sullivan."

I shook my head at the moniker. "I just want a quiet life."

It was my mantra and I just kept saying it.

Brody laughed. "You picked Mary Millard for a bride. An heiress like that comes with... complications."

"And she's anything but quiet," Parker added, adjusting his

cock. He was probably thinking about how she was a screamer. The knowing smile from Miss Rose this morning as we'd said our farewells was indication enough our actions hadn't gone unnoticed.

"And Laurel was any less complicated?" Andrew asked Brody. While neither Parker nor I had lived at Bridgewater when Laurel, Brody's wife with Mason, was discovered in a blizzard, we knew her story. She had a rich father like Mary—not *as* rich as Mary's though—and he'd planned to marry her off to a miserable man. It had been a dangerous time for her, but that was behind the three of them.

Brody grinned and shook his head. "Even with that mess resolved, she's still a handful."

"It wasn't simple for Emily or Elizabeth either," Kane added, referring to two of the other brides on the ranch.

Parker came over and slapped me on the shoulder. "We all picked... tempestuous brides."

The men nodded and shared a conspiratorial look. While Bridgewater men cherished their brides, we were also very dominant lovers and gave our wives what they needed, not always what they wanted. Just like the ass plug this morning. Mary had resisted it at first, then, remarkably, came as I slowly worked it in and out of her, training that tight ring of muscle to relax and open.

"This isn't about you, remember," Kane surmised. "It's about Benson besting you. As you said, he doesn't know you're Shooter Sullivan, only the man who stole his bride."

"That's Mary," I said. "Our stolen bride. We have our plan against his expected retribution?" I asked.

The men nodded, having spent over thirty minutes working

through some options and coming to a group decision on how to end Benson.

"The plan is a good one," Andrew said. "The question is, will your bride understand?"

MARY

"Sully and Parker," Laurel said, looking at me with a mixture of awe and admiration. "They are quite the pair. Handsome, too."

"Laurel," Mason warned.

When we arrived at Bridgewater, I hadn't known what to expect. Sully and Parker had told me on the ride that it was a ranch run as a community—slowly turning into a small town of its own—where everyone helped its success and growth. With additional friends joining frequently, additional land was purchased, new houses built. Families made. The last included Sully and Parker since they returned with me. If they kept fucking me as they had, we'd be making our own family in about nine months.

They'd been surprised at our marriage, but from what they said, I wasn't the first to just arrive wed to two of the Bridgewater men. Emma had been—amazingly—bought at an auction by Ian and Kane and married directly after. Elizabeth had been a mail-order bride to a mean man and surreptitiously wed to Ford and Logan instead. Ann had married Robert and Andrew on a ship. All marriages they'd told me about were quick and with quite a tale to go with them.

As for me, *I* was still getting over the surprise of being married myself. Of the unswerving attention of two men. I was surprised they'd let me be dragged to the kitchen where the lunch was being prepared.

I'd been told all the meals were communal, cooked and served in Emma's house. When we arrived, introductions were made, but because of the large group, I feared I would not remember everyone's names for some time. I was the new one though, and they questioned me continuously about myself and then about my men. *My men.*

"Are you interested in the attentions of other men now, wife?" Mason asked Laurel. "Other men who are claimed by Mary?" While he eyed his wife, he carved a chicken on a large platter. There were three of them to be done and he was making fast work of it.

Laurel smiled at him sweetly. He laughed, knife in hand. "That look gets you spanked, love."

Spanked? Laurel was spanked too?

She waggled her eyebrows at him. "I know."

Based on her response, she seemed to like it… and want it. Just like me. I'd been surprised at first when Parker had spanked me, but I'd liked it. No, I'd loved the feel of his hand on me. I'd loved the attention I was receiving. I'd loved the way all thoughts fled my mind and I just focused on Parker and his touch. On Sully and his carnal words.

A baby fussed in a cradle beneath an open window. Laurel's focus shifted and she went over and picked up the infant.

"Tell us about yourself, Mary. Not your men," Emma added. She was at the table, a baby in a special chair beside her. The little girl smacked her tiny palms on the table and watched as a green bean fell to the floor. A brown dog, sitting smartly below, snapped it right up. The baby, of course, giggled at the dog.

"If you hadn't heard, I'm a Millard."

All the adults in the room—Emma, Mason, Laurel, Ann, and Rachel, or was it Rebecca?—nodded.

"This is like a small town, news spreading so quickly."

"There aren't any secrets here," Ann said. She was helping her toddler son wipe his hands. It seems the children ate before the adults, at least today. It was hard to keep from grabbing a chicken leg and nibbling, for it smelled so good and I was quite famished.

Laurel laughed. "Mmm, how can there be secrets, Mason, if you and Brody fuck me on the front porch?"

Mason lifted his head from his work and grinned. "You were a cranky lass and needed it. If you keep up this tone, you'll be spanked out there—" he pointed out the back door to the porch, "—while everyone's eating."

The smile slipped off Laurel's face and she looked contrite. Mason winked at her, then went back to slicing the chicken.

I couldn't tell if the duo was joking or not. Mason would spank her on the back porch of Emma's house where everyone could see—and hear?

"Yes, I'm quickly seeing that everyone knows everything," I commented, thinking I needed to ask my men where they'd spank me if they felt the need. "My father owns one of the copper mines in Butte. My mother died when I was little and he was not the most... loving of parents. I was raised a society miss and ultimately expected to make an advantageous match."

I was handed a slotted spoon and a large bowl and pointed in the direction of the stove. "Thanks—"

"Rebecca," the woman said.

"Yes, Rebecca." I turned to the stove and started scooping small red potatoes from the steaming water and placed them in the bowl. "It's not Boston or New York, but in Butte, society is important nonetheless. So is business. My father made a business arrangement with Mr. Benson and I was the traded commodity."

"I know Benson. He's... not very nice," Mason said, pausing as he cut the chicken.

I could only imagine what he would have said if he hadn't tempered his words.

"It doesn't matter now, because I'm married to Sully... and Parker." I skipped the details of the brothel, for how could I explain it all without seeming either a whore or just downright strange? While it seemed everyone was very open-minded, I wasn't ready yet to offer all my secrets.

"Sully and Parker, they're quite the pair," Laurel said, circling back to the beginning of the conversation.

Parker and Sully came to mind as I put the new potatoes in the bowl. I wasn't sure if it was the steam or thinking of what they'd done to me this morning that was making me hot all over. Rubbing my legs together, I felt my bare pussy, slick and smooth with no hair. My arousal and their seed coated my folds, the lips of my pussy and it was so noticeable now. Even my ass. Oh God. Sully had coated the plug he'd confiscated from Chloe and carefully worked it inside me.

I'd been up on my knees, cheek pressed into the bed as he'd taken his time. Breathing hard, I'd panted and pushed hard, relaxed as he praised me.

Such a good girl. Breathe. Yes, push back. Ah, you're opening so nicely. Look how you stretch so well. Think of our cocks sliding in, how it's going to feel when we take you here.

When the plug had finally been seated inside me, I'd slumped into the bed, adjusting to the strange feel of the foreign object. I felt open and filled. Besides that, I felt... controlled. Every part of me belonged to them. I should have hated it, for Benson would surely control me if we were wed. This was different. So different that I came from Sully's attentions. The men had been surprised and instead of punishing me, they'd praised me.

But, that wasn't it. The plug was in, but Sully had said, "We're not done, sweetheart. The training's just beginning."

The clatter of a spoon pulled me from my thoughts. I felt *everything* now, including my sore ass. Parker had pulled the plug from me before we left The Briar Rose, but I still felt the effects of their efforts. It was all even more noticeable since I wasn't wearing a petticoat or drawers. I was bare to the air down there. Completely bare. They could just lift up my skirts and.... I did flush then. It definitely wasn't because of the steam.

I had to wonder what they planned to do with me next. While Mason had said he and Brody had fucked Laurel on their front porch—where everyone could have seen and heard—I had to hope my husbands wouldn't do that. But when we went to their house—our house—I knew there would be no reprieve.

10

ARKER

For a week, we kept Mary in our house. Naked. The only adornment she was allowed was a plug in her ass and our seed on her thighs. A week of keeping her well occupied as we waited to hear news so we could implement our plan to finish Benson once and for all.

Quinn and Porter had gone to Butte with their wife Allison. While there, they'd enjoy the theater and other offerings of the big city, and at the same time, keep an eye on Benson. None of them had been there before and would not be a threat, or connection to Sully, for Benson. After six days, they finally sent word that Benson was coming after Sully. We'd been right, he'd paid henchmen to complete the task for him and they were on their way to Bridgewater.

The knock on the door came as we were in the bedroom

with Mary. She was riding Sully, her hands in a tight grip on the slats of the headboard, her ass stretched and filled with a plug much larger than the one Chloe had given her. With gentle coaxing, she'd been able to go up two sizes in the past few days and she was close to being ready for us take her at the same time. While it was something Sully and I longed to do, we were in no rush. I loved seeing the look on her face as we taught her new things. She was as insatiable as we were, not inhibited in the slightest, and *very* sensitive, easy to arouse and come.

I pulled on some pants and went to the front door, Mary's little gasps and moans followed me down the hall as Sully talked dirty to her.

Kane took off his hat and came inside. As the sound of a palm against bare flesh carried to us, Kane raised an eyebrow. When Mary cried out, he grinned.

"I'm interrupting."

"Sully can tend to her on his own for a bit."

"Yes!" Mary cried, her voice desperate and breathy.

I adjusted my hard cock, grinned shamelessly.

"I'll make this quick then. Porter sent word. Benson's men are headed this way. I've told the others. We'll leave in two hours."

I nodded, pleased it was finally time to take care of Benson, although I wasn't too keen on leaving Mary in this moment. Although, we were always hard and eager for her, so there really never was a good time to part from her. Sully had wanted a simple life, and hopefully, with Mary's issue with Benson soon resolved—or Benson's issue with Sully—we could return to the ranch and fuck in peace for the rest of our lives. We needed this to end.

"Who's staying behind?" I asked. The women would be protected.

"Dash and Connor, plus Mason. Quinn and Porter are returning with Allison this afternoon."

"Good."

Mary screamed then, and not in pain.

"Two hours?" I asked, eager to shut the door in Kane's face and get back to my bride.

"Make it three." Kane slapped me on the shoulder and let himself out.

Returning to the bedroom, I found Mary in bed, eyes closed, her skin coated in a sheen of sweat. Her pale hair was a wild tangle on the pillows and she was trying to catch her breath. Sully sat on the side of the bed, tugging on his pants. He arched a brow in tacit question, and I nodded in reply.

He stood, did up the buttons. While he had the look of a well satisfied male, his focus had shifted to Benson.

"Mary," I said, my voice gentle.

She looked so sated, so well satisfied, that I knew my next words were going to ruin that for her. Hell, I didn't want to ruin that for any of us. She slid her leg over the sheets, tucking it up at an angle. Did she know her bare pussy was now open to us? Did she know it was deliciously pink and swollen, coated in a thick layer of Sully's seed? Did she know the handle of the plug in her ass parted her cheeks so invitingly?

If she did, she was a vixen and she would be spanked.

"Mmm?" she replied.

"We have something to tell you." Sully's voice wasn't as gentle as mine—it never was—and she opened her eyes.

"Benson is sending men here, to come after Sully," I said. There was no way to soften the words.

"What? Now?"

She moved up onto her hands and knees, her eyes wide with fear. Shifting a bit, she moved so the plug wasn't uncomfortable. Her breasts swung prettily beneath her and I ached to cup them in my palms.

"Here, sweetheart. Over my lap and I'll take that plug out."

I moved to sit down and she held up her hand to stop me.

"A plug in my ass is not what I'm thinking of right now. You said Mr. Benson is coming here for Sully, then... he'll do what? Take me away?"

We both shook our heads.

"No." Sully put his hands on his hips, lowered his head. "You have no value to him while married to me."

Mary looked thoughtful, bit her lip. "He's after you."

Sully nodded once.

"You're going to stay here with the women. Mason and a few other men will remain behind to protect you."

Her eyes narrowed. "You're going to leave me here?"

She'd become comfortable in her nakedness, but I doubted now she was thinking about how she looked, all lush breasts and bare pussy, sitting on our bed. It only made my answer come that much easier.

"Hell, yes."

"But—"

Sully crossed his arms over his chest. "We protect what's ours. That means you. You'll stay here where we don't have to worry about you, where we can take care of Benson and come back to you."

"Yes, but—"

"Do you want us to fuck you some more before we leave or

punish you?" Sully asked, his tone that of when he'd tossed Mary over his knee before.

"I get no say?"

"In this?" I asked. Absolutely no fucking way. "No. It is our job, our privilege, to take care of this, of Benson. Once and for all."

"How long will you be gone?"

I moved to sit beside her, pulled her so she sat across my lap, carefully settling because of the plug. Tucking her head beneath my chin, I reveled in the soft, lush feel of her. I wanted this, I wanted *her*, without complications, without worry looming.

This, holding her, was peace. It was simple, quiet. Perfect.

"We will draw them away from Bridgewater, so the encounter will not be today. I imagine three, four days."

Her hand stroked over my belly absently. She'd teased me before and it had not been like this. At times, she could be a little vixen. Now was not one of them. Nonetheless, her caress made me hard. *Everything* about her made me hard.

"You will go and stay with Laurel and Mason."

I stroked her silky hair, which was a wild tangle all the way down her back and over my thigh.

"All right," she replied.

Relieved, I kissed the top of her head.

"We have a few hours. Kane was impressed with how hard you come. Do you think you can scream like that for me?"

She stiffened in my embrace. "He heard?" she asked, worried.

"Mmm."

Using two fingers, I tilted her chin up so she met my gaze. "Just for you?" she asked.

"For me and Sully. While we're gone, you're going to have to continue to use the plugs on your own."

Her brow furrowed.

"When we come back, we're going to claim you."

"Together," Sully added.

"That's right. Onto your back, legs nice and wide." I helped her settle into position and damned if I didn't want to crawl between those thighs and fuck her. But that could wait.

"Pull that plug out and we'll get you the next size up. You'll get it all slicked up and put it in yourself. You'll wear it until lunchtime, then again when you go to bed."

Sully must have seen a look in her eye, for he said, "We'll know, sweetheart. When we get back, we'll be able to slide a finger inside of you, nice and easy to check, then our cocks."

Sully held up the new plug, longer and thicker than the one inside her now, and the jar of slick lubricant. "If you put that new plug in quickly, we'll have more time to fuck you before you go."

"You... you want me to do it myself?"

"Yes, we need to know you can do it while we're gone," Sully replied. "Then we'll fuck you. It'll be so nice and tight."

"And I want to hear you scream at least twice so I can think of your pleasure while I'm gone," I added, knowing the nights on the trail were going to be long. Thinking of her would help.

I sat down on one side of Mary, Sully on the other, and we held her knees apart, watching as she tended to her ass training. When her nipples tightened and her skin flushed, I knew it was far from a chore.

11

ARY

I lay awake that night, thinking of my men. They were going to somehow come upon Mr. Benson's hired men, lead them away from Bridgewater, then ambush them. How that was going to make Mr. Benson decide that I should no longer be his wife was beyond me. The man wasn't going to stop until Sully was dead and I was a widow, eligible for marriage once again. If Sully and the others killed the men who were coming for him, Benson would only send more. The numbers would not stop.

There would be no end. None of the peace and quiet that Sully was looking for. I just wanted Sully and Parker to have what they wanted. Unlike Mr. Benson's desire, it wasn't a tangible thing, not something you could buy. It was a way of life and I craved it, too. I didn't need money, I just needed my men.

There was only one way to stop Mr. Benson. The idea came

to me as I stared at the shadows dancing across the wall in Laurel's extra bedroom. The soft curtains in the window shifted with the summer breeze and picked up the glint of the moon. I was alone in a strange bed and a strange house. I'd become familiar with sharing a bed with two big men, adjusting to being held all night, pressed between two warm bodies. Now, I felt alone. Even on the warm night, I was chilled. I longed for my men.

I hadn't thought about what Chloe had said about Mr. Benson's mine that morning in the washroom at the brothel. Sully had come in and interrupted us and then introduced me to a razor and an ass plug. To say that my thoughts had been occupied by them since was gross understatement. But with them having been gone all day, I'd had time to think.

Mr. Benson's mine was dry. There was no copper. That meant no more money, no more lavish lifestyle. No wonder he wanted me. He wanted my money, and ultimately my father's mine. There were no shortages of copper coming from it. The vein was a good one. A deep one.

Being married to Sully meant my father's mine was unattainable for Mr. Benson. He was desperate. This meant that he wouldn't stop trying to get to me. He wouldn't let Sully remain alive. The longer the time that passed, the more desperate he would become. Sure, he could find another heiress, but I was the only one in Butte who was—or had been—unmarried and of marriageable age.

Lillian Seymour was forty-six and had seven children. If her husband died, Mr. Benson could wed her, but his intentions would be obvious. The woman was toothsome, and seven children?

There was Olive Morris, but she was twelve. I doubted Mr. Benson had six years, let alone six months to wait.

I was his only chance.

I knew how to end this once and for all. It wasn't through Sully. It wasn't even with hired thugs. There was one person who needed to learn the truth and stop the business deal. My father.

I had to get to Butte. I had to go see my father, tell him about Mr. Benson's mine. Then I could live my life with my men without fear or danger looming over us. And one of my men was in danger. While they'd said it was their job to protect me, it was my job to save them. I knew how to save Sully and I couldn't just sit with Laurel and the other women with that information and do nothing.

Butte was only a few hours away. An easy ride for a horse with a light rider. No one was after me. *I* wasn't the one in danger. I just had to figure out how to get away. Mason, Quinn, Porter and the other men were very protective. *Overly* protective. I rolled onto my side, tugging the blanket about me, thinking. When the sun began to rise, the sky changing to gray, then a perfect pink, I had my plan.

SULLY

"What the fuck do you mean she's gone?"

I was sweaty and tired and dirty and all I wanted to do was

see my wife and sink into her. But no. No, my wife had left a note saying she was going to Butte.

Butte!

I'd left Parker in the stable with the horses as I went to Mason's house to retrieve Mary. We stood on his front porch and I glanced to the south as if I could see her and that God-forsaken town. Once I got her back, we were never going to that town again. Shit.

Mason scratched his head, looked a mixture of furious and befuddled. "She came to breakfast, ate with us like everything was fine. She told me you'd tasked her with training her ass and needed some privacy."

I wasn't shocked that Mason knew about Mary's task while we were gone. I was shocked that she'd told Mason about it. While she was completely uninhibited with Parker and me, she was very shy when it came to sharing what we did with anyone else. Just knowing that Kane had overheard her come while I fucked her the other morning had been mortifying for her.

Everyone at the ranch knew we fucked. Everyone at the ranch knew we fucked with abandon. We all did. We spanked and sucked, licked and fucked our wives. We even trained their asses because not only did we like a good ass fucking, so did our brides. We all especially liked fucking our own bride at the same time.

This was something we had yet to do with Mary, but I'd hoped to accomplish that today. Not now.

Now I had to go to Butte to get my wife.

"We took care of Benson's men, sent one back to him alive with a message."

The heavy gallop of a horse came toward us.

Parker jumped from his horse before it even stopped, searching the covered porch. "Mary's in Butte?"

"Shit, yes," I muttered. The other men who stayed behind all knew she'd gone and one of them must have told Parker.

"Fuck. Butte?" Parker shouted.

"Mason was telling us she told him she was going to go train her ass and needed privacy. Next time he checked on her, she was gone."

Parker stilled, eyes wide. "That woman, when we find her, is going to find out all the ways we can train that ass."

He put his hat back on his head and walked over to his horse, grabbing the reins.

"Quinn went after her. Once we knew she was gone, he followed. But it's a big town and I can't say if he'll find her easily."

"Oh, we know where to find her," I muttered. I took the steps two at a time and practically ran to the stable.

12

ARY

"Are you sure you should be doing this?" Miss Rose asked.

I was once again in the kitchen of The Briar Rose sitting across from the woman who was more mother than madame. This time I wasn't an innocent virgin, eager for some titillation. A week with Sully and Parker had stripped all innocence from me and I was glad for it. I loved everything I did with them, that they did to me, that they commanded I do to myself. I even liked the dratted ass plugs.

"It's my fault that Sully is in danger. He doesn't want to be another target, whether it's gossip or rumors or bullets. He just wants... quiet."

"It's not your fault," she countered as she stood to fill her mug from the coffeepot on the back of the stove. When she held the pot toward me, I shook my head. I was jittery enough as it was. Voices drifted from the floor above. It was early afternoon and while everyone was awake, no one moved too quickly. Nora had come down for a cup of coffee, said hello, then left. The butcher had delivered a box of stew meat for the evening meal, but otherwise, we had the kitchen to ourselves.

"Benson would have gone after whatever man you married."

I frowned. "That doesn't make it any better. Whomever I married—if it had been Parker instead—would have been Benson's nemesis."

"You don't think Sully can defend himself?"

"I do." Both my men could defend themselves, and me. "But while they went out there to protect me from those... goons Mr. Benson sent, it doesn't solve the problem. He'll just keep sending more until one of them gets lucky and kills Sully."

I felt sick just saying those words.

Miss Rose reached across the table and took my hand. "You really love them, don't you?"

I laughed, but sadly. "I've known them a week. They kept me naked almost that entire time!"

Miss Rose didn't look horrified, only humored. "What's wrong with that? It sounds romantic to me."

"Romantic? Do you have any idea what they did to me?"

She smiled, shook her head. "Oh, I have some idea. I'm sure you can give Chloe some lessons now."

I tugged my hand away and folded both of them in my lap. "Yes, I suppose I could. But love? I'm not sure what I feel is that. I don't want anything to happen to them. I don't want anyone else to have them. I want to... please them."

Miss Rose laughed and lifted her coffee cup in the air as if to toast me. "Mary Sullivan, that's love."

I looked up at her hopefully. It was love? This... need to take care of them, to give them what they wanted? They'd said it was their privilege to protect me and I understood that now. It was my job as their wife to protect them when I could. Knowing what I did about Mr. Benson could protect Sully. I wanted him. Needed him. *Both* of them. But love? "Really?"

"Your mother, God rest her soul, would have told you just that. Your father, well, he's a man and an idiot."

Very wise words.

"And I have to face him. What time is it?"

"Half past two."

I stood and carried my mug over to the sink. "He will be home at four, as usual, I'm sure. For once, I'm glad he's so fastidious."

"Until then, you'll sit here and tell me about your men. I want to hear all the salacious details."

PARKER

"Oh, you two have got your hands full with that bride of yours."

Miss Rose stood at the back door of the brothel, not even allowing us to enter.

"Let us in and we'll take her off *your hands*," I told her.

We'd ridden hard from Bridgewater and went straight to the brothel. Oddly, it was her shelter in this crazy town and I knew she'd be safe there. Elsewhere, I had my doubts. But Benson didn't want her. Well, he wanted her, but only if she was marriageable. That wasn't happening any time soon.

"She's not here. That's why I'm not letting you in. I'm saving you time."

"Shit," Sully swore, walked in a circle. "She's gone to Benson."

I was ready to go over to his house, his mine or wherever the fuck his was and rip his head off with my bare hands. If he touched or even breathed near Mary....

"Benson? No."

I frowned, confused. "Then where the fuck is she?"

Miss Rose raised one delicate eyebrow.

"Pardon the language, but we need to find her so we can spank her ass."

She smiled then, looked between the two of us.

"We'll make her safe, *then* we'll spank her ass," Sully clarified.

"She went to see her father," Miss Rose said. "She knows something, gentlemen. She refused to tell me what it was, but it was something that will ensure Benson leaves you alone."

I was so frustrated I wanted to throttle her for the answer, but this woman, hell, I saw Mary in her. Or her in Mary. Stubborn, headstrong, smart. Fucking logical.

"Then why go to her father? The man couldn't care less about her."

She put a hand to her chest. The layers of white ruffles were almost blinding in the sunshine.

"She wouldn't tell me. But Millard's house is easy to find. Just go to Granite Street. His is the biggest."

MARY

"Hello, Father."

My father looked up from his newspaper and his eyes widened in surprise. He wore his usual black suit, crisp and sharp at any time of day. His gray hair was neatly combed, his jowls still covered his shirt collar. Sitting as he was in his usual wingback chair, his rotund physique was even more noticeable. Perhaps it was my perception of him that changed, being with Sully and Parker, two well-muscled giants. "Mary."

His tone was neither angry nor happy. He was neutral, as usual. I brought about no inspiration in the man, no happiness. In fact, the only time I'd seen him show true emotion toward me was anger when he'd discovered I'd married without his consent.

"Where is your husband? Don't tell me he abandoned you."

Oh. There was the Gregory Millard I knew. I stood before him just as I had all my life. First with a nanny, standing in my nightgown and robe bidding him goodnight. Then older, with my tutor reciting what I learned that day. I always stood feet together, back perfectly straight, chin up, hands clasped together in front of me.

It wasn't comfortable. It was practically subservient, but it was familiar. If I was confronting him, I wanted to be at ease, at least as much as possible. That was why I chose this time of day. He always read the newspaper before dinner was served at five in the dining room. He did not have a meeting, did not entertain. This was his time to read the news. Nothing else. Except today, when I would confront him for the first time.

"You didn't think he would have lingered longer than a

week? I am a copper heiress, after all. If I remember correctly, you told me I was the richest woman in the entire Territory."

"You would still be if I hadn't struck you from my will."

I shouldn't have been surprised, but I was. Perhaps it was more by his haste as stripping me from his life than his ruthlessness. I'd always had hope that maybe he'd change his ways, turn into a kind and attentive father. Loving. That would never happen and I had to let go of that. I had Sully and Parker and they were enough. They gave me everything I needed and it was nothing money could buy. It was love.

"Then it's a good thing that I'm not here for money."

He folded his paper precisely and placed it in his lap. "Why are you here? You've made your bed."

Yes, yes, I had. I thought of our bed at Bridgewater, Sully and Parker asleep on either side of me. I was naked and both of them had a hand on me, even in sleep. I was sheltered and protected, cherished… and yes, loved. I just hadn't known what love was before I met them, before Miss Rose helped me see what it really was. With a father like the man before me, I'd never known.

"I'm here about Mr. Benson."

"Oh?"

"You are aware of his reasons for marrying me?"

"Of course." He sighed. "Mary, I do run the largest copper mine in the world. Your assumptions belittle your intelligence, not mine."

His insults were not very subtle, but I pushed through, for this was important to me. To Sully. To all three of us.

"Are you aware that the Beauty Belle mine is dry?"

He laughed and shook his head, admonishing me and shaming me at the same time. "Dry? Impossible."

I would not be cowed. "Then why did Mr. Benson want to marry me?"

"We are merging the two mines' businesses to reduce employees and to improve efficiencies. We do not need two medical stations or food depots if we are one organization."

That was a sound business idea and I could offer no argument.

"Whose medical station would close?"

"His, for it is smaller."

I nodded slowly, relaxed my hands. I was right. My father was smart, but Mr. Benson was more cunning. "And whose food depot will close?"

"His, for it is further from the train depot. It will cost less to deliver the goods to mine."

"And what would Mr. Benson gain from this arrangement?"

"Besides you?" He looked at me directly, his gray eyes piercing.

"Besides me, what does Mr. Benson gain from your business arrangement?"

"We each gain twenty percent share in the other's mine interests."

I nodded my head as if thinking about his words. It was as clear as crystal, at least for me. "And when you die, who would inherit?"

"If you had wed Mr. Benson, you would have."

"Meaning, he would have inherited it all since a wife can hold no property. A wife's worldly possessions belong to her husband. I'd say the arrangement is quite in Mr. Benson's favor."

"Explain your insinuations again?"

"They are not insinuations, they are fact." It was hearsay,

but I wasn't going to tell him that. "The Beauty Belle is dry, meaning you would a gain twenty percent share in nothing. As for Mr. Benson, he would gain a twenty percent share in your mine, which is thriving. You don't need any shares of his company, for you do not face bankruptcy and are quite solvent, but in this arrangement, all you would lose is that interest in *your* company."

"How would you know something like this? Who told you? You can't know of business dealings like this!"

My father tossed the paper on the floor, pushed to his feet and stepped closer. His gait was slow, for he was grossly obese and his gout was surely inflamed again.

"You forget, Father. You are the one who had me educated so well."

13

ARY

"I don't believe a word you say." His face turned mottle red and he used the back of his hand to wipe spittle from his chin.

"You should," Mr. Benson said, stepping into the room.

I turned to face him, my skirts whipping about my ankles.

"Benson! Have you heard such lies?" my father asked.

Mr. Benson eyed me shrewdly. The dark anger was still there, in his eyes, the tenseness of his jaw, in every line of his body. I also saw the cunning he'd hidden so well before. Gone was any artifice of caring or concern, for myself or my father.

He closed the door behind him, turned the lock with a loud snick. I took a step back, knowing that the man was unhinged and I was truly in danger. My father hadn't realized it yet.

"Actually, Gregory, your daughter is very astute. The Beauty

Belle is dry. I'm barely pulling enough from her a day to pay the bills."

Father's eyes widened and I worried for his health. I'd never seen him so angry, so out of control. "This is preposterous. You're bringing in a million a day!"

"You are," Benson countered. "I'm bringing in as much as a two-bit whore on Broad Street. It would have all worked out, if not for you."

He shifted his focus from my father to me. Knowing the arrangement was dead, that he would not be owning a portion of the Millard mine, he wanted retribution.

I took another step back, held my hands up in front of me. "You had not declared yourself and I met Mr. Sullivan while I was in Billings. It was very romantic."

"Romantic? You talked of fucking on the train platform."

Father moved back, stumbled over an ottoman. A lamp teetered, a small clock tipped and fell over.

"He is my husband, Mr. Benson. I am allowed to have... sexual congress with him."

"Yes, of course you are. But he is not here? Where, pray tell, is Shooter Sullivan?"

He knew where Sully was, knew that his paid men were laying siege to kill him. I just had to have faith that Sully and Parker, the other Bridgewater men, were more skilled and outmaneuvered them. I had to hope they were all safe.

I had *not* expected to have Mr. Benson arrive at my father's house. I'd intended to tell my father of Mr. Benson's plan, warn him so he wouldn't follow through. Simple, really.

Except...

"You married Shooter Sullivan?" my father asked, clearly stunned.

"Yes, I did."

"She married a Bridgewater man," Benson told my father. "Do you know what that means?"

I flicked a glance at my father. I'd rather him hear the truth from me than from Mr. Benson. I was proud to be married to both men. I would not diminish it by making it seem tainted. "It means I married Shooter Sullivan *and* Parker Corbin. Two men. I married both men from the train."

My father stilled, his face blank. "You... I mean... I don't understand."

No, he wouldn't.

"It means Mr. Benson wants Sully dead. If that occurred, then I'd be a widow. Marriageable. He wouldn't need your business arrangement to get the Millard money. I've been the key all along."

"Yes, you little bitch, you ruined everything!" Mr. Benson's eyes narrowed. Sweat beaded on his brow and he began to stalk me across the room.

My father sought shelter behind his large desk.

"Ruined everything? I did nothing. I lived my life how I wanted it. For once, I didn't do what my father bid, what was expected of me. I married for love, to not one man, but two. They love me and cherish me, and yes, fuck me. But that's what marriage is, not an *arrangement*."

My heart was hammering in my chest and I began to shake.

"I wanted the business deal, yes," Father admitted. "But I thought Mr. Benson was a good fit for you. Clearly, I was wrong."

Mr. Benson grinned, his teeth gleaming as bright as the whites of his eyes.

"Mr. Sullivan is dead." His words held a dark vehemence.

Their Stolen Bride

He was so sure of himself that my faith in Sully was beginning to waver. What if... "I've taken care of him."

No. He couldn't be right. Sully was too good at being... Sully. He had Parker with him, the other men from Bridgewater, too. I slowly shook my head. "You're wrong. You've been watched. We knew your men were coming."

"What men?" my father asked, dropping down into his desk chair.

"Men hired to kill her husband," Benson snapped.

"With the last of your money?" I asked. "It was wasted. Sully's not dead."

"You are a fool. No man, not even Shooter Sullivan, could survive the O'Malleys."

I'd never heard of them, but that didn't mean much. I hadn't heard of Sully's reputation either and he was so gentle with me. Unless he wasn't and then he was tossing me on the bed and... oh. I couldn't think about that. Not now.

"You are coming with me until I have official news of his demise. Then we will wed. No church ceremony, a Justice of the Peace will suffice."

"I'm not going with you." I backed into a side table; a porcelain figurine fell to the wood floor and shattered.

His anger radiated from him. "That bastard, Sullivan. He *stole* you from me! You are mine. The money is mine. Your father will not stop us."

A horrible sound rent the air and we all spun to look at the door. It had been locked, but now it slammed into the plaster wall with a harsh thud, then bounced off. The doorframe was splintered, ruined.

I jumped and gasped, even Mr. Benson took a step back.

Sully stood, big and brawny, in the doorway. His head

almost reached the top of the doorframe. He stepped into the room, gun in hand. "Her father might not stop you, but I fucking will."

God, he looked so good. I raked my gaze over every inch of him. He appeared whole, healthy. Perfect. He was *not* dead. Elation and relief made me giddy.

Parker came in behind him, then Kane. The three of them were so big, the room suddenly felt tiny. But Mr. Benson was desperate and quick.

He grabbed me by my wrist and tugged me into him. The thick scent of hair tonic was cloying. With one arm banded about my waist, he wrapped his hand around my neck. Squeezed. His grip was tight, a little too tight. I could breathe, but barely. My eyes bulged and I clawed at his grip with my fingers. Panic set in. Sully and Parker had their eyes sharp and fixed on Benson but didn't move any closer.

Why weren't they helping? Grab him! Do *something*. Wheezing, I shifted and tried to wiggle from Benson's hold, which made him laugh, the sound maniacal.

"Oh really? One twist and she's dead." His hand squeezed a little tighter and I made a gurgling moan. My nails dug into the top of his hand, in his wrist, but he was strong.

Sully looked beyond angry, but I couldn't focus on anything or anyone. Not anymore. Only Mr. Benson's tightening grip.

"Let her go," Sully said. I'd never heard his voice so angry. "You want me dead so you can marry her. She holds no value to you dead. Besides, you can't kill me if you're holding her."

Mr. Benson's hand loosened a bit and I could breathe. I gulped in air, relaxed slightly in his hold. It seemed silly not to fight him, but I was too interested in catching my breath.

"That's a start," Sully told him.

"You're holding the gun on me, Shooter. I'm not stupid enough to release your wife. You'll just shoot me."

Sully held out his hands from his sides, walked sideways to a small table, laid the gun down. "There now. I'm not going to shoot you."

Mr. Benson relaxed his hold even more.

"Benson!" Father cried.

The man turned instinctively toward my father and as he did so, took a half step away from me.

A deafening gunshot had me jump, then cover my ears.

My father's voice was flat. "He's not going to shoot you, I am."

My father's gun was smoking and I was slow to understand that he'd shot Mr. Benson. As that became clear in my befuddled mind, the man fell to the floor, solid, dense. Dead.

"Fuck," Parker muttered.

Sully ate the distance between us and tugged me right into his arms. I felt the beating of his heart against my cheek, felt his warmth. Knew he was alive. He was kissing the top of my head, holding me so tightly I could barely breathe, but this time, I didn't care.

My ears were ringing from the single gunshot, but I heard Parker speak.

"Are you insane? You could have killed her!"

"I might be old," my father replied. "I might even be a bastard when it comes to my daughter, but I'm a very good shot. That man threatened Mary and he deserved to die."

I lifted my head and looked at my father. He'd never once said he loved me. Never hugged me, told me he was proud of me. Nothing. But his killing Mr. Benson proved that somewhere in his heart, he cared about me.

"Father..."

He shook his head, put the gun on the desk. Kane came around to stand beside him, surreptitiously taking the weapon away. I doubted my father even knew he'd done killed a man. He was in shock as much as me, perhaps more. Not only did he discover his daughter hadn't run off to get in bed with a stranger, but he discovered his business partner was dirty and intended to commit several murders.

He'd been wrong. He'd been wronged. I didn't expect an apology or anything from the man. But I could give him something.

"Thank you, Father. Thank you for saving me."

I looked up at Sully. His eyes held so many emotions. Anger, fury, fear, lust and anguish.

"Let's go home," I told him.

He nodded once, then turned us toward the door. I doubted he would let me out of his arms anytime soon. I was just fine with that.

"Mary," my father called. Kane still stood near his desk, perhaps to ensure he didn't do anything else reckless. "I'm sorry."

Sully pulled me out of the room and down the hall. I wondered if it was the last time I would be in this house, if my father was rid of me once and for all, but I wouldn't worry about that now. Now, I would find that peace and quiet with Sully and Parker.

14

ULLY

It had taken three hours for the sheriff to be summoned, inspect Benson's body and for us to be questioned about the incident. Millard's money and standing helped, and no one was thrown into jail before being questioned. While her father might be an asshole, he'd ensured Mary was kept outside and away from the body, as well as the first to recount to the lawman what had occurred. Parker, Kane and I offered our information next, and quickly, too, for Millard was insisting Mary had been through enough and that I take her home. He'd said she could succumb to hysteria from her ordeal. While I doubted a bout of that, it showed the man had at least one caring bone in his body.

It had taken three more hours to ride back to Bridgewater. She'd sat in my lap the entire journey, but remained quiet, even falling asleep with her cheek against my chest. I'd calmed during the journey, becoming more at ease the further we distanced ourselves from Butte, the longer I held her. On the ranch, everything was quiet and Mary was safe. Unless she went off on some harebrained idea again. Before the day was out, Parker and I would ensure she would never do something like that again.

Standing outside the front door, I took in the peaceful view —prairie grasses waving in the soft breeze, snow-capped mountains in the distance. The only sounds were the grasshoppers and the wind.

As Mary walked hand in hand with Parker to the house, I knew I was right where I belonged. I was with my family. By marrying Mary, we'd become just what I'd always longed for. Soon, we'd make the family even larger. I wanted to see Mary become round with child. *Mine.* Ours.

Very possessively, we took our bride directly to the washroom. As I began to fill the tub with water from the sun-heated cistern, Parker helped her out of her clothes. When she'd stripped off her dress, I made note that she wasn't wearing her petticoat or drawers. It pleased me that she followed that dictate even while we'd been gone.

We bathed her then, Parker and I kneeling at either side of the tub, using soap and our hands to wash away the dirt and filth of the day.

"Why are you being so nice to me?"

"Should we drown you instead?" Parker asked, running a cloth over her pale shoulder.

She looked down at the water. There were no bubbles, only the scent of roses that came from the bar of soap in my hand.

"I thought you'd be mad."

"I was angry," I admitted. "The journey home has tempered it."

I hadn't just been angry. I'd been frustrated and afraid and... fuck, so many emotions had roiled through me. When we'd walked in Millard's house and heard the crash from the hallway, we'd followed the sound of raised voices. There were more than two people in that locked room, meaning it wasn't just a little father-daughter discussion. Our bride, in the invariably short time we'd known her, had never been one to throw tantrums, and I doubted she'd have started then. I'd given Parker a quick glance, and he'd nodded, his jaw tight. Only a door separated us from Mary. Lifting my leg, I'd kicked right beside the doorknob, forcing the wood to splinter around the solid lock.

The sight before us when the door had slammed open... fuck.

"We were so scared that something had happened to you. Then Benson—"

Parker didn't say more than that, just had Mary tilt her head back so he could wash her hair. In that position, I could see that her neck held no marks from the attack.

"Better?" Parker asked, wringing the water from the long strands of her hair when he finished.

I'd just been content watching.

She nodded, gave us a smile. "Much."

"Good, then it is time for your punishment," I said as I stood, grabbing a bath sheet from the nearby stool.

"Punishment?" Mary asked, looking up at me, a frown creasing her brow.

She looked perfect. Whole. Unharmed. Her hair was a wet mass over one shoulder. Her cheeks were bright with color, which was much more agreeable than earlier when they were pale with shock. Beneath the surface of the water, her body was so pale and lush. Her nipples were plump and full, and lower, I could just discern the glint of pale curls at the top of her pussy. I ached to sink into her body, to lose myself in her. As Parker stood, he shifted his cock in his pants and I knew he felt the same. It was time to take her together, to claim her fully. But that had to wait.

"Why should I be punished?"

I held out the sheet and after Parker helped her from the tub, I wrapped her in it. She took the ends and pulled them across her chest, but the fabric became instantly damp and clung to her every curve.

"Why?" Parker asked. He stripped, then climbed into the tub. "Your note only said you went to Butte. Butte! We didn't know where you were and had to go to a brothel to find you. Out of every woman in the Territory, you should know the type of men who frequent that place."

He grabbed the unscented soap and scrubbed his body.

"I've been safe every time I went in the past," she countered, watching Parker's hands at work. "Up until I married you, I lived in Butte. I never went about chaperoned once I left the schoolroom."

"In the past, you weren't married to us and were not under our protection," I added, moving to sit on the bench beneath the window to tug off my boots. "Going to the brothel alone is not your only indiscretion. You traveled all the way to Butte by yourself, then went to confront your father. Again, alone! You were unprepared for the worst consequence."

Parker stood and stepped from the tub. He grabbed another bath sheet and began to dry himself.

"Do you have any idea what could have befallen just on your journey to town?" Parker put the towel on the hook to dry and put his hands on his hips. He didn't reach for his clothes. They wouldn't be needed in the bedroom. "You could have been thrown from the horse. A rattlesnake bite. Outlaws!"

I wasn't too keen on used water, but I wanted the dirt off of me before I fucked Mary and I was in a rush. Quickly, I climbed in and scrubbed.

"I didn't know where *you* were when you went away either, and you were to be gone for days," she countered, her words full of her own anger. "You went with others, but you were going against outlaws. Outlaws! They carry weapons. I only went to see my father. My *father*."

"Your father's an ass and has acquaintances who are ruthless," I said, rinsing away the soap. It was a quick bath; only a rinse in a frozen creek was done faster.

"We are both military men," Parker told her. "So are all the other men at Bridgewater. We know how to shoot, how to fight an enemy. Plan for contingencies, bad outcomes. Hell, even floods. It was our job. Protecting the innocent *and* fighting the enemy is what we've all been trained to do. Going against Benson's men, we weren't going in blind. There were six of us and the men who stayed with you knew the plan, knew where we'd be."

I climbed from the tub and dried myself.

"I was well armed," she argued. Her chin had gone up and the color in her cheeks now wasn't from the bath. "I had the truth. Hard facts about Mr. Benson that would have ensured my father wouldn't do business with him. That would have ensured that Mr. Benson would want nothing to do with me. I was *free*."

"Why didn't you tell us about these hard facts?" I asked. When she'd recounted her version of the incident to the sheriff, we'd learned then about Benson's mine and his reasons for being so desperate to marry Mary. "We could have gone with you to your father."

"I learned of them from Chloe, but you two shaved my pussy and put the plug in my ass directly after. I got distracted and forgot about it until after you left."

"You're going to be distracted again. Right now. Drop the sheet."

Mary did as Parker commanded, letting the damp covering slip to the floor. There wasn't any way she could miss our hard cocks, although they were always hard around her and she'd accustomed herself to it.

He took her hand and led her to our bedroom. I followed, enjoying the view of her perfect ass sway as she walked, even the little dimples just above.

"Here's what's going to happen," Parked continued, going over to the dresser and picking a plug from the wooden box where they were kept, then the jar of ointment. "You're going to show us how you can work the plug into your ass, because if you've been a good girl, you've been doing so while we were gone. Then we're going to spank you and you are *not* going to come."

"We know how much you like to be spanked and we know how much you like things in your ass. That is far from punishment for you," I added.

"You will deny me my pleasure?" she asked.

"You will know then how we felt when we discovered you gone. Frustrated, out of control. Needy."

Their Stolen Bride

"Then we're going to claim you, Sully in your pussy and me in your ass."

We stood, patiently waiting for Mary to come to terms with her fate. The plug would go in her ass—we had to ensure she was truly ready for us to take her together—and she would be spanked.

"Would you like a warm-up spanking first before the plug?" Parker asked.

Of the two of us, I was the more commanding. Mary came to me when she wanted to be fucked up against the wall or over the kitchen table, rough and hard and quick. When she wanted a gentler ride, she found Parker, riding his cock or grabbing the headboard as he pressed her into the bed as he took her. *He* was the softer one, the soother. But now, after what we'd witnessed today, Parker was the one who would ensure she learned her lesson.

Pursing her lips, she looked at both of us, at the plug in Parker's hand, then sighed. She took the hard object and crawled onto the bed. Parker sat on the edge and unscrewed the jar's lid as she settled onto her back.

"I'd rather you do it," she admitted. She wasn't missish. She didn't act all virginal or embarrassed by the carnal things we did together. She told the truth. She liked a plug in her ass and she liked when we took control. What she didn't realize was that while she was putting it in herself, we were very much in control.

Putting one hand on her knee, Parker flared it out and Mary let her legs fall open. Her perfect pussy was on display.

I stood at the foot of the bed, my hands gripping the rail of the footboard and watched. It was almost impossible not to climb onto the bed and just sink right into her. She was wet, I could see her folds shiny and slick. She'd be so warm, so soft and she'd wrap around my cock so perfectly, her body milking the cum from my balls as she came.

"While we were gone, I thought of you here in our bed, using this plug all by yourself," Parker told her. "Was it hard to put the largest one in?"

"At first. It just took a little while," she admitted.

Parker groaned. "Thinking about you here, talking deep breaths as you pushed it in slowly. I'm going to come just thinking about it. You're going to show us just how you did it."

15

ULLY

She must have realized that it would please us, or that she held power over us with her body, for she took two fingers and coated the plug with the slick lubrication. Pulling her knees back toward her chest, she moved the plug into position, pressing it against her puckered rosette.

Someone could have knocked on the door. Hell, a tornado could have taken the house away and neither Parker nor I would have known. Just watching Mary fill herself with that plug, fuck. It didn't go in easily, but Mary breathed through it, pushing then pulling it back, then pushing again until it stretched her wide, then popped into place.

Her feet fell to the bed and she sighed. I stared. She'd taken the largest plug, which meant she could take our cocks. We could claim her as ours... finally.

"Good girl," Parker said once she was done. He tested the seating of the plug and she moaned. Her blush spread from her cheeks, down her neck and over her breasts. A slight sheen of sweat coated her skin. Satisfied, he gave the plug a light swat, eliciting a gasp from her lips. "Stand by the side of the bed. Bend over so your forearms are supporting you."

Carefully, she shifted and moved from the bed. Once she was standing, Parker took a pillow and placed it at the edge so that when she leaned forward, the extra height lifted her ass in the air and into the perfect position.

Her cheeks were flushed, her hair was half dry and curling wildly down her back. Her nipples were tight little peaks and her eyes were lust-filled.

"We've married a naughty girl," Parker said, stroking his cock. "She likes that plug in her ass, Sully. Are you ready for my cock to claim you there?"

Mary eyed Parker's tight grip on his shaft, how he stroked it, rubbing the pearly drop of fluid into the head with longing. She whimpered. "Yes."

Parker stood and stroked a hand over her smooth flesh. I came about and saw the plug's handle parting her cheeks, her pussy directly beneath it on perfect display. "Then let's get this ass nice and pink first."

With a hand on her back, Parker guided her so she was in just the right position.

I groaned, cock in hand. My balls tightened and I squeezed around the thick crown trying not to come from just looking at her. "You're so beautiful, sweetheart. We love that you're such a naughty girl. *Our* naughty girl."

Parker's hand cupped one side of her ass before he lifted it. She tensed, knowing what was coming, but still gasped when his palm connected. An instant handprint appeared, brilliantly pink next to white.

"Parker!" she cried, glancing over her shoulder at us. Her hands were clenched tightly in the blanket.

He grinned. "Like that, do you?"

She narrowed her eyes and glared. "Yes, and you know it."

He spanked her again, in a white spot that was just begging for color. "Enjoy it all you want, but don't come."

Parker took her to task then, spanking her slowly but methodically.

"How much does she like it?" I asked. Parker moved his hand away and I immediately slid my fingers over her folds. I could see they were wet, but feeling that slick heat, sliding two fingers inside her and having her walls clench down was almost too much to bear. Mary moaned and tossed her head back in obvious need, but I couldn't give it to her. There was a lesson here she needed to learn first, so I pulled my hand away.

"She's dripping," I said, my voice gruff with my own need.

"Please," Mary gasped.

Parker gave her another spank. "What do you want?" he asked.

"You."

That word. God, that word. It was ruthless and sweet, tempting and perfect. Perhaps Parker was made of sterner stuff, for he said, "Not yet."

He spanked her some more and it quickly became clear that Mary was on edge. She could come from a spanking alone, although the plug in her ass certainly helped. Her body was so sensitive, so responsive to us. She wanted *everything* we did with her.

"I... I need. I can't stop—"

Parker lifted his hand away. "You can. You will. You may not come."

"Why?" she cried. Tears slid down her cheeks. Her hair was mostly dry now and clung to her face and back in a sweaty tangle.

"Do you need us?"

"Yes!"

"Are you frustrated?"

Mary sobbed then, tried to turn, but I put a hand on her back. We were at the crux of our lesson now and it was time she knew I was just as involved in this as Parker. He'd spanked her, but this was about all of us.

"Of course, I am. You won't let me come!"

"This is how we felt, sweetheart, when you left the note," I said. "When we knew you went alone. We were so frustrated."

"We needed you and you weren't there," Parker added.

"We were out of control. Helpless. Desperate."

She slumped onto the bed then, crying. "I'm sorry."

I sat beside her, the bed dipping, and pulled her onto my lap. She gasped as her reddened bottom pressed against my thighs, but she wrapped her arms about me and cried.

Parker sat next to us, stroked her hair.

"I was left out. Separate." Her words were difficult to discern through her tears, so I just held her and ran my hand up and down her back until she calmed some.

"Tell us," Parker prodded.

"We went to the brothel on my suggestion and you trusted my destination. We weren't married then, but I felt like I was included in the decision making. About *us*. But with Mr. Benson's men, you just left me behind."

"It was dangerous," I said. "You'll not be placed in danger, ever. We will not sway on that."

"Yes, but I'd liked to have been involved. While those men needed to be handled, the solution was a simple one. One that I could have accomplished with you."

Mary's concerns were valid. While we would never compromise her safety, she was smart and should be included in any problems that we encountered. Together.

Parker glanced at me. He could read my thoughts, it seemed, for he said, "Then we must communicate better. We must include you in conversations about activities that may be dangerous."

"That doesn't mean you will *participate* in the activities," I clarified.

"In return," Parker added, tilting her chin up so she met his eyes. "You will never go off on your own like that again. As we said, you left a note, but the journey was not one even the men here at Bridgewater would take alone, and never without a gun."

"All right," Mary replied. "I'm sorry. I really am. I see why you were upset, why I was punished."

I kissed the top of her head, breathing in the scent of roses. "Later, you will apologize to Kane as well."

She nodded, her head bumping against my lips.

Parker stood and I leaned forward, pushing Mary onto her back and leaned over her.

I observed her tear-stained face, her eyes that were so clear, so pale. Her skin was still flushed, her arousal only diminished, not dampened. "Now, you said you needed something from us?"

Heat flared in her eyes and a brilliant smile spread across her face. She shook her head, which made me frown.

"I don't need something *from* you. I just need you." She lifted a hand in the air toward Parker. "And you."

"You have all the money in the world and yet you want something that has no value and is freely given," I murmured. "You amaze me."

She lifted her hand and stroked over my hair and cupped my neck. "No value? I think what we have, what we share together, is priceless." She turned her head and looked up at Parker. "I'm ready."

Parker squatted beside the bed. "Yes, you are. You're ready for your men."

"You're ours, Mary," I added. "It's time to claim you. Together."

16

ARY

My body tingled all over. My ass was scalding hot and throbbed from Parker's spanking. He hadn't gone easy on me, for he was not doing it as play. It was punishment, pure and simple. Regardless, my body still reacted, still ached for more, still hungered. I *liked* it when they were rough. I *liked* it when they spanked me. I *liked* it when they put their fingers inside of me. I did not like being unable to come. I'd been so close, but they'd somehow known, sensed that I was on the brink, and stopped. Again and again I was taunted with the brilliant pleasure, but denied.

I'd felt frantic, desperate, out of control and so damn frustrated. I understood how they felt when I'd left a note and gone to Butte. Yes, they were overprotective and domineering, but I'd been reckless. I didn't want to feel that way again, didn't want *them* to feel that way again.

With Benson dead... I shuddered. He was evil and I couldn't believe Father had shot him. Perhaps there was more to the man, more to the two of us than I ever knew, but now was not the time discover it.

Now it was time to be with Parker and Sully. Together. I'd continued to stretch and train my ass for their cocks and with the largest plug deep inside me now, I knew I could take them. I wanted to take them both.

I *needed* it. I *needed* them.

There was only one thing I could say, the one word they were waiting eagerly to hear. "Yes."

With that one breathy word, I was lifted and maneuvered on the bed as if I weighed nothing. Sully settled on his back, his head on the pillows, his body laid out like an offering. An offering I was more than eager to take.

My pussy clenched with the need to be filled with that massive cock. Clear fluid seeped from the slit of his cock and ran down along the thick vein that pulsed up the length. I knelt on the bed, Parker a hard, hot body at my back. He cupped my breasts and ran his thumbs over my nipples as I drooled over Sully's cock. I needed it. I needed to taste that pearly drop, to feel him hot and thick in my mouth.

I told him so.

Sully's eyes turned even darker, flared with heat.

Parker's hands released me and I leaned forward, grasping Sully's cock in my grip, then flicked my tongue out and tasted him, tasted his essence. Salty and pungent, it coated my tongue and I wanted more. That little drop was for me. All for me.

Opening wide, I took the flared crown into my mouth and sucked it. Sully's body tensed and he swore beneath his breath.

I couldn't see what Parker was doing, but I felt the bed shift. As I took a little more of Sully into my mouth, I felt Parker's big hands on my thighs, insisting I part my knees. There was no way I could take all of Sully's cock into my mouth, so I began to stroke my grip up and down his shaft as I lifted and lowered my head. His hand fell into my hair and tangled there, holding me in place. I was doing something right.

When I felt Parker's tongue on my pussy, licking along my seam and then up to my clit, I groaned. That, of course, made Sully groan.

"Do that again, Parker," Sully said. "Whatever you did, her moans are pulsing up my cock."

Parker flicked my clit, then sucked it into his mouth. I moaned again, and Sully groaned.

"She was so wet from the spanking, I'm just licking her all clean. So we can get her dirty again." Perhaps it was Parker's words, or perhaps I was pushing Sully too close to the edge, but he gently tugged on my hair, lifting me off his cock.

"I want my cock buried deep in your pussy when I come. Straddle me."

Parker gave me one last lick, then a kiss on my inner thigh, before straightening.

I lifted my leg over his flat stomach, my hands on his upper chest for balance. The hot feel of his skin, the soft prickle of the hairs there, made me aware of how big he was. All man. He was virile and dangerous. Potent and powerful. And yet I'd reduced him to groans of pleasure with my mouth on his cock.

We could reduce each other to the basest of beings, lost

only in what the others were doing. We craved, we needed, we gave.

Lifting up, I rose above his cock and settled back down, that tasty crown nudging my entrance. I was slick and wet and so eager for him. Pushing myself down, I felt my pussy lips spread and part for his cock, stretching open as he began to fill me.

My head fell back at the exquisite feel of him. Hot inside me, hot beneath my palms, hot against the inside of my thighs. Lower and lower I sank until I was fully seated astride his lap. As I did so, the plug in my ass nudged his thighs and I gasped. I was so tight, so crowded full of cock and hard plug.

It wasn't enough. I wanted more. And so I began to move. Up and down I slid, shifting and rotating my hips, ensuring that my clit rubbed against him just right. My eyes fell closed and I moaned. This was what was missing during the spanking. I'd been empty and now I was so filled.

Parker's hand slid down my spine, then back up in a smooth caress. "Lean forward, sweetheart."

Collapsing my elbows, I lay down on Sully's chest, our skin slick with sweat. My nipples felt abraded against his chest. His hands cupped my hips, held me in place as he kissed me. Tongues tangled, breaths mingled. We were truly one. But one wasn't enough.

I had two husbands and I was desperate for Parker, too. With a gentle tug, he began to pull the plug from my bottom. At first, it opened me wide and I gasped against Sully's mouth, but it easily slid free and then I felt empty.

Whimpering, I shifted my hips. More. I needed more.

"Shh," Parker soothed.

Sully's mouth moved to the line of my jaw, my neck as I felt the bed dip, felt Sully shift his legs to make room for Parker.

Without any more delay, I felt the flared head of his cock nudge my trained ass. It was slick and hot, insistent, a completely different feeling than the plug.

Sully continued to kiss me as his hips canted slightly, allowing my inner walls to be stroked and nudged by his cock while keeping me in place for Parker.

The pressure of Parker's invasion grew and I broke the kiss with Sully. I could only breathe and feel secure in his hold with his hands on my hips. Parker gripped my shoulder and I felt grounded. I was between them and soon filled by both.

All at once, my body gave up the fight and his cock slid past the tight ring of muscle that had been trained to accept it. I groaned at the thick feel of him; he pulsed and was warm, hard and yet soft at the same time. He moved in, then retreated, deeper and deeper until he, too, was fully seated.

We were all breathing hard, sweat coating our skin. This wasn't some virginal sex act. This was dark and naughty, yet loving and the most intimate of acts. I was allowing these two men to claim me, to take me together. While they were the ones in charge, I was the one with all the power. I was the one who united us, in body and soul.

And so when Parker's cock was seated completely, I could do nothing but relinquish all control. I was theirs, pinned between them, filled with their cocks. Impaled, stuffed. Taken. There were so many words, so many emotions for how I felt to say aloud, so I just put my head on Sully's shoulder and breathed.

As Parker began to slowly retreat, Sully nudged his hips, driving him a touch deeper. When he pulled back, Parker filled me. They worked in tandem, opposing forces at work to drive me to the brink and then over.

It wasn't hard to do. I'd been primed by their punishment—Parker's belly smacked against my tender bottom as he took my ass. There was no forgetting their dominance in all things. I was sensitive and eager, my orgasm right there, so brilliant and bright, so dark and greedy.

I wanted it. I needed it. I needed everything my men gave me.

"Take it," Sully said, as if he could sense how close I was.

"Yes!" I gasped.

"You're ours, Mary." Parker's voice was a rough, guttural sound.

"Yes!" I repeated.

Yes, yes, yes.

I needed to be filled, claimed, fucked. I needed to be pinned between the two of them, for that was where I belonged.

"Can I come?" I asked. I wanted their permission, wanted to give them everything. My control was all that I had left and once they gave their affirmations, it was gone. I handed it to them like my body, my pussy, my ass, my heart.

"Now, sweetheart. Come now and I'm going to fill you up."

"Yes. Come and squeeze our cocks. Milk the seed, take it deep."

The waves of pleasure and need were too great. I succumbed in one tense, bright burst of light. My body tensed, my scream trapped in my throat. All I could do was clench and squeeze, hold my men deep inside me, to work the seed from their body in the most elemental of ways.

Sully's grip tightened on my thighs and with one last thrust, he groaned. Hot seed pummeled my insides, spurt after thick spurt. Parker immediately followed, that grip on my shoulder tightening and his cock pulsing deep inside me.

Their seed coated me. Marked me. Made me theirs. There was nothing left between us. No barriers. No walls. No dastardly plan.

We were free.

I whimpered when Parker pulled out, sighed when Sully slid free, but snuggled into them as they moved on either side of me. I was still between them, still had their hands on me. Nothing would separate us. I had physical reminders of this—a stinging bottom, surely some bruises forming on my hips, seed slipping from me, but I didn't even need any of it, for I had their hearts and they had mine.

WANT MORE?

Read an excerpt from Their Brazen Bride, book 8 in the Bridgewater Ménage Series!

EXCERPT - THEIR BRAZEN BRIDE

ABIGAIL

"I will kill her now—" Paul Grimsby cocked the gun, the sound of it making me jump. "—or you can save her. You decide."

He had the look of a man not to be trifled with. Tall and lean, he seemed as if he'd been stretched on a Medieval rack. His curly hair was tamed with pomade, and the cut of his suit was the latest fashion. But he was anything but a gentleman. Especially since he held a gun to my friend's head.

I glanced over my shoulder at the man, one of Mr. Grimsby's oversized and brutish lackeys, who blocked the room's only exit.

"What...what is it you want from me, exactly?" My voice was shrill with nerves. Sweat trickled down between my breasts. I wrung my hands as my knees practically knocked. I hadn't been invited to the Grimsby house, I'd been *accompanied*

Excerpt - Their Brazen Bride

by the man at the door and another who had ventured off somewhere in the big house. The journey across Butte from my finishing school was only ten blocks or so, but it had felt interminable. I'd spent the time considering ways to escape them; I was walking down a busy street. Screaming I was being kidnapped was at the top of the list of possibilities. But the two henchmen who'd flanked me had warned if I so much as waved to someone on the street, my school friend Tennessee Bennett would be killed.

I remember the first time I met her, commented on her unusual name. She'd said her parents named her and her two sisters after states. Georgia and Virginia were fine names, but she'd been burdened with Tennessee, a definite mouthful.

"Money, of course," he replied evenly. A clock on the mantel over the fireplace chimed the hour. The room was so civilized, but the conversation was anything but.

It seemed Mr. Grimsby had every intention to do so. Kill Tennessee, that was. Shockingly, he'd already killed her father who'd come in town for the school's graduation and to accompany her back to North Dakota. Mr. Grimsby had no remorse, no conscience. I glanced at Tennessee, sitting stiffly in a high-backed chair, her usually bright complexion now matched a bed sheet. She looked at me with pleading eyes, tears streaming down her cheeks. She'd gotten herself into this predicament, and had pulled me in unwittingly as well. Eager for a suitor, she'd been bold with her attentions for Mr. Grimsby, one of the more successful and wealthy businessmen in town. Not only was he rich, but attractive—she thought him so, where I'd found him quite unappealing—and, most importantly, a bachelor.

Excerpt - Their Brazen Bride

Eager for money over love, she'd wanted to land a rich husband but had lied to Mr. Grimsby about the wealth and station of her family from the very beginning. She wasn't a railroad heiress as she'd said, simply a second daughter of a banker from Fargo. The guise was innocent enough and done by many a woman throughout time to improve her lot in life, but Mr. Grimsby seemed to want Tennessee's nonexistent inheritance more than the woman herself. He wasn't as rich as he seemed, either. If he weren't a madman, they'd make a perfect match. But when the truth came out about Tennessee's perfidy, he'd become enraged; her father's dead body left in the street and the black eye on her face were indication of this.

And the gun pointed at her head.

"I don't have money," I replied, wetting my lips.

"You don't have looks, but you've got money."

Mr. Grimsby's eyes narrowed on my cheek with something akin to revulsion, and he shook with rage. I was used to being taunted about my scar, but I was glad he had not found any kind of attraction to me as he had Tennessee. She was beautiful, poised, and gentle hearted. "I know your background, your brother. You might not have cash on hand, but he has one of the largest ranches in this corner of the territory."

I was surprised he wasn't forcing *me* to marry him instead. If he wanted money badly enough, he would overlook the scar. But no. He was too vain for the likes of me and wanted a beautiful bride. Tennessee. Not me. For once, I was happy to have been disfigured.

"Land and cattle. That's all he has," I replied. "I can't bring you a cow."

I bit my lip, knowing it wasn't the right thing to say, for he while he dropped the gun from Tennessee's head, he closed the distance between us and grabbed my arm. I cried out at his cruel hold. Flinched.

"I don't want a fucking cow," he hissed, spittle flying. "I want money or something to sell *for money*."

"All right," I replied. What else could I say? He'd killed Tennessee's father to punish her for her lies. What was keeping him from lifting the gun to my head and pulling the trigger? "I'll... bring you something to sell."

He released his hold, wiped his mouth with the back of his hand with the gun.

"You have a week." He turned and pointed at Tennessee, who was now crying in earnest. "One week and then I kill her."

I nodded numbly, my heart beating frantically. I was going home anyway now with graduation behind us. I wasn't sure how I would be able to return, but I'd worry about that later.

"If you don't come back, my men will find you." He waved the gun in front of my face, and my eyes followed the lethal weapon.

I retreated a step. He didn't do anything, so I took another tentative one, then another, afraid to turn my back on him. Tennessee was still crying.

"Don't leave me here!" she cried, holding her hand out to me to take.

It hurt to leave her behind, but if I was going to save her, I had to go. I heard the door open, and it was only then when I turned. The henchman held the door for me and escorted me out into the street, my friend's sobs following. I had to help my friend. I had to return home and find something I could bring back to appease Mr. Grimsby. Something James wouldn't miss. Otherwise, she would die. And if I didn't do it in the week, he'd send someone after my brother. I'd saved him as a little girl. I couldn't let him die now.

GET A FREE BOOK!

JOIN MY MAILING LIST TO BE THE FIRST TO KNOW OF NEW RELEASES, FREE BOOKS, SPECIAL PRICES AND OTHER AUTHOR GIVEAWAYS.

http://freeromanceread.com

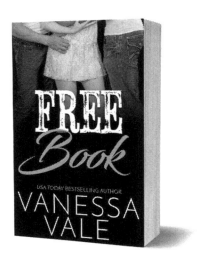

ABOUT THE AUTHOR

Vanessa Vale is the *USA Today* Bestselling author of over 40 books, sexy romance novels, including her popular Bridgewater historical romance series and hot contemporary romances featuring unapologetic bad boys who don't just fall in love, they fall hard. When she's not writing, Vanessa savors the insanity of raising two boys, is figuring out how many meals she can make with a pressure cooker, and teaches a pretty mean karate class. While she's not as skilled at social media as her kids, she loves to interact with readers.

www.vanessavaleauthor.com

ALSO BY VANESSA VALE

Bridgewater County Series

Ride Me Dirty

Claim Me Hard

Take Me Fast

Hold Me Close

Make Me Yours

Kiss Me Crazy

Mail Order Bride of Slate Springs Series

A Wanton Woman

A Wild Woman

A Wicked Woman

Bridgewater Ménage Series

Their Runaway Bride

Their Kidnapped Bride

Their Wayward Bride

Their Captivated Bride

Their Treasured Bride

Their Christmas Bride

Their Reluctant Bride

Their Stolen Bride

Their Brazen Bride

Their Bridgewater Brides- Books 1-3 Boxed Set

Outlaw Brides Series

Flirting With The Law

MMA Fighter Romance Series

Fight For Her

Wildflower Bride Series

Rose

Hyacinth

Dahlia

Daisy

Lily

Montana Men Series

The Lawman

The Cowboy

The Outlaw

Montana Maidens Series

Claiming Catherine

Taming Tessa

Dominating Devney

Submitting Sarah

Standalone Reads

Western Widows

Sweet Justice

Mine To Take

Relentless

Sleepless Night

Man Candy - A Coloring Book

The Alien's Mate: Cowgirls and Aliens

Manufactured by Amazon.ca
Bolton, ON